I0524450

THE
SECRET
TOMB

N GRAY

VINCI
BOOKS

Vinci Books

vinci-books.com

Published by Vinci Books Ltd in 2025

1

The publisher and the author have made every effort to obtain permissions for any third party material used in this book and to comply with copyright law. Any queries in this respect should be brought to the attention of the publisher and any omissions will be corrected in future editions.

A CIP catalogue record for this book is available from the British Library.

Paperback ISBN: 9781036702151

The EU GPSR authorised representative is Logos Europe, 9 rue Nicolas Poussion, 17000 La Rochelle, France

contact@logoseurope.eu

By N Gray

Scout Thorne

The Secret Tomb

Murder of Crows

Blaire Thorne

Ulysses Exposed

Voodoo Priest

Butterflies and Hurricanes

Salvation

Underworld Legacy

Shifter Days, Vampire Nights, & Demons in Between

Twisted

Lady Hawk and Her Mountain Man

Hidden Shifter

Wolf

Wolf Retreat

Night Hunter

The Fixer

Kai

Lee

Flynn

Jude

Chapter One

Victor stood beside his older brother and watched the madman show them how they could use the mask. But the real reason for the demonstration—they needed to determine whether it was the right mask. Harry 'Houdini' Morris pulled the cart closer so they could see clearly.

The darkness of the night never bothered Victor, he thrived in it. He did his best work at night, using the shadows to blend in, but tonight his eyes scratched, and the blackness troubled him for some unexplained reason.

Victor's older brother, Seth, was as impatient as a young child waiting anxiously for Father Christmas to deliver his presents.

"Father is going to get a kick out of this," Seth said, grinning from ear to ear. His emerald-colored eyes sparkled like jewels in the starless sky. "He's been looking for this mask for centuries."

Victor rolled his eyes. It was true, their father, the King of the Underworld, had been looking for the mask, but only because he wanted to destroy it. Their father was afraid of anything that posed a threat to his power, and their father didn't want to lose his position within the supernatural world. Which was understandable. Neither did Victor nor his brother.

Harry made an exaggerated show of draping his coat over his shoulder and crouched behind the old cart. The action reminded Victor of the good times when there was no electricity, and gaining souls for his pleasure was easier. He, too, walked around in a long black coat and top hat, enticing men and women with delicious sins for their pathetic soul. These days, it was all about the latest electronics or immediate gratification that created the shortest attention spans.

Harry coughed, gaining Victor's attention. Victor smiled knowingly; it seemed he too had a short attention span.

Harry slowly opened a large vintage wooden chest held within the cart. "My Dark Lord's, thank you for meeting me here," he said, gesturing at the ancient cemetery. "It's rare my Lord's venture out of the Underworld, but I assure you tonight will be worth your while."

"Just get on with it, human," Victor snapped, his eyes burning red. "Before I eat your soul."

"Yes, my Lord," Harry muttered and stood straighter. "We found the mask that was once lost," Harry said, pulling a never-ending cloth out of his pocket. "It wasn't easy to find, and we had casualties. When my men found this hidden in a secret tomb, I knew who the rightful owners were—"

"You weren't interested in the riches that could come with finding such an artifact?" Victor asked suspiciously. His left eye itched as he watched Harry with the cloth and wondered why the distraction. "You could've auctioned this off to the highest bidder."

"Oh, no my Lord," Harry said, sweeping his arm low and bowing down. "It is not riches I'm after." He stood up and continued pulling the never-ending cloth out of his pocket. Once done, he threw the cloth on the ground but kept the ring that was tied to it.

"Then what do you seek?" Victor asked. His tone was louder and harsher than normal, making Harry flinch.

"Only to serve," Harry said, averting his eyes. "I wish to serve the Dark Prince's in the Underworld and when it is time, you will ensure my family gets what they deserve." Harry's eyes flitted to Victor and then to Seth before staring at the ground once more.

"Why?" Victor's suspicion grew. Nobody willingly gave something away for free, along with their soul. Was this charade only so that he could exact revenge on his family? It made little sense.

"I assure you," Harry said, glancing at Victor. He stepped closer to the dark angel, whose black wings had opened and now spread wide, displaying his power over the human. "My time here has ended, and I wish to become a servant in your world. I honestly have had enough of this world," he swept his hands wide, "I'm sixty-seven and my tricks are old in these times. Nobody wishes to see an old man perform magic tricks. I can do nothing about my parents for sending me to that institute when I was a boy. They thought I was special when I was not. I only loved doing magic; that was what made me special. But my wife and kids are alive and well. I wish the worst to happen to them," Harry said maliciously as his eyes filled with hate and narrowed.

"Ah, there it is. You wish revenge on your family?" Seth asked, nodding. "They treated you unkindly?"

"Yes, my Lord. They were cruel all my life. They never

supported my shows or appreciated the life I'd given them. No matter how many hours I worked, the street corners I performed tricks on, did my family say thank you. Ever. And I think it's time they all got what they deserved."

Seth clapped his hands slowly, creating a sonic boom sound. "Deal, now let's get on with the show."

Victor glared daggers at his brother, who shrugged in response. "You're far too trusting, brother. If anything happens, it's your fault."

"Yes, yes, as it always is." Seth waved Victor away like he did when they were children and nodded curtly for Harry to continue.

Victor stared suspiciously at Seth.

Harry called someone over who had been lurking in the shadows of a tree. It surprised Victor because he hadn't seen that person until they walked across the lawn. He was usually more aware of his surroundings and could tell the difference between hidden dangers and shadows. He tugged on his shirt, glancing over his shoulder and then back at the assistant as he approached the magician.

The assistant wore a matching red coat that billowed out behind him as he walked toward Harry. The assistant was younger than Harry, but that meant nothing; some supernaturals never aged at all, and from this distance, Victor couldn't tell what he was. The assistant held open his hand, and an orb glowed blue in his palm; he was either a wizard or a warlock. When he closed his eyes and said an incantation, Victor heard and understood what was about to happen; he was going to raise the dead at their feet.

The ground vibrated, and the headstone near the necromancer toppled over. The sand dispersed, creating a hole big enough for the corpse to animate and sit up. But before the dead could rise, Harry removed the mask out of the wooden chest and slapped it on the necromancer's face.

Two things happened at once; the corpse crumpled back inside its coffin like a dirty old rag. And the necromancer's shoulders dropped when the orb disappeared, and he glared daggers at the magician.

"There we have it, my Lords; The Mask of Immortality or the opposite when used on any supernatural, rendering them powerless," Harry said. His smile widening as he removed the mask from the assistant.

Harry's eyes flitted from the brothers to the mask, and then something happened in slow motion. He raised the mask as if to praise it, then lowered it onto his face.

Harry grew twice his size, fell onto all four limbs as he shifted into something much bigger. He didn't stop growing as he morphed into a gigantic wolf-orca hybrid; a killer whale on land. He swished his large, dark tail backward and forward. His head turning toward Victor and growled hungrily like a wolf.

Victor didn't have time to transport himself back to the Underworld, and he didn't have time to call for help as Harry 'Houdini' Morris lunged for him.

Chapter Two

Ralph ran to my right-hand side and away from the action. I stopped running and yelled, "Why are you going that way?" I shrugged when he turned to look at me. "The corpse went this way." I pointed at the nearby shed, the door banging shut.

"You go that way, I'll go this way," Ralph said sarcastically with a roll of his eyes. His wavy brown locks held tightly in a ponytail. Every couple of years, he'd either shave his hair close to his head or grew it long, reminding me of a grizzly bear; like now. "Didn't your mother teach you various maneuvers to get the dead guy?"

"Ha, funny." I rolled my eyes. "But you're going far off, buddy. The dead guy went inside the shed."

"That's what you think," he sang and continued up the stairs and into the house. "I'll flush him out," he yelled. "Be ready with those deadly palms of yours."

"Fine," I yelled. "I'll just catch him here," I grumbled to myself, pulling my gloves out of my pants pocket and slipping them on. I crept toward the shed and slowly opened the door; the sun behind me casting the small room in enough light to see. "Where did you go, you zombie?" I mumbled to myself.

"Scout!" Ralph shouted.

I spun around in time to see the animated corpse reach for me, its beady black eyes dripping pus while the rest of his body losing chunks of rotten flesh in its wake. I couldn't believe I missed him. For a dead guy, he was pretty smart and quick on his dead feet.

"Aaaaar," mumbled the corpse. His head flopping from one side to the other while he growled with lips that were no longer there. He only had a few teeth left after the fight that had put him in the grave, and those few stood in different directions.

"Not today, buddy," I said, shoving my palms into his chest.

The corpse grabbed my wrists, its slimy grip tightened.

"Ew, you're so gross." I gagged, then pulled a face when a chunk of green, rotten flesh fell on my new sneakers, which angered me. "No," I screamed as I pushed my power into his chest, pushing the corpse backward.

Heavy footsteps stomped down the stairs and approached me. The corpse's soul flew out of its body as Ralph stopped beside me, out of breath, and sprinkled salt around us. The salt wasn't always necessary, but we needed it because the animated corpse was so volatile. And to my other side, Blaire, my mother, ran up to us, whispering an incantation, keeping the soul out of its body. The incantation was necessary but sometimes I'd forget to say it. When that happened, I had to work harder, pushing their souls out of their bodies.

I whistled a specific tune. The ghostly figure of the ferryman appeared in his phantom boat, scooped up the silently screaming soul, and continued on his merry way. His eyes glaring at me from the back of his head like it did every time. I no longer shuddered or glanced away, instead I waved and smiled.

I let go of the corpse and his body crumpled to the ground, and dusted my gloved hands. After flicking off chunky pieces of the corpse, I carefully removed the gloves. "All in a day's work," I said, beaming.

"Good job, my child," Mom said, kissing my cheek. "But don't relax too much. We have another case," she thumbed behind her at Ralph's vehicle. "I suggest we grab something to eat before heading that way."

"Good," Ralph said, grinning. "I'm starving."

"You're always starving," I chortled, smacking his abdomen. "What's the other case?" I asked, slipping my gloves into a plastic bag. They'll need to be dry-cleaned before I could use them again, but I had another pair in the car.

Ever since I started working with Mom and Ralph at Ulysses Assassins, the need not to touch those we were after became greater. There was something about me shoving their souls out of their bodies that made me feel queasy, but wearing gloves seemed to remove the nausea.

"It's at the aquarium. There's an issue with their new orca," Mom said, scratching the left side of her chest until it became inflamed. "And a village in Peru just vanished," she said absentmindedly as she scrolled upward on her touch-screen phone. "Weird things are happening around the world," she rambled, still scratching her chest with her free hand.

I reached for her and stopped her from scratching. "You're about to make yourself bleed," I said, pointing at the raw skin.

"Blaire seems to be allergic to the new detergent as well," Ralph chimed in. "Come, I need food."

Lately, my mom had been struggling with allergies; first it was tomatoes, then her shampoo, and now it's her detergent.

"I'll be fine. I'm seeing Mel later," Mom said with an urgent need to scratch.

"Stop it." I chastised her like she used to do to me. "You can't see Mel now?" I asked. Mel was a werewolf and the doctor for every shifter in Sterling Meadow. She was great at what she did, and the wolves didn't seem to mind sharing her with every supernatural. Years ago, when they formed the Were-Animal Alliance—the WAA—, Sterling Meadow became one of the safest towns for shifters and supernaturals to live in. Even the vampires didn't seem to mind working with everyone.

"She's busy with the leopards," Mom said, rubbing the inflamed area with her index finger.

"You probably can't put anything on that right now? It might sting the crap out of you." I winced looking at the reddened area.

"I'll be ok," Mom said, slipping her arm through mine, and resting her head on my shoulder. We walked in silence toward Ralph's vehicle, but before I opened my door, a warm wind caressed my cheek and all the hairs on my body stood on end.

Mom let go of me and spun around with her weapons drawn, ready to use it. I unsheathed my knife, glancing around for the attacker. Unfortunately, Ralph was very human and human slow. He noticed nothing until he turned around and saw us standing like we were ready to strike an invisible force.

Tiny blue sparks flickered at my fingertips, ready to blast this creature approaching.

In the distance, a tall, dark figure approached with a dog running beside him. I eyed him narrowly and mumbled his name.

"Who?" Mom asked, ready to pull the trigger.

The blue sparks at my fingertips died down like an ice-cold bucket of water washing over me and my heart stuttered in my chest. My breath caught in my throat, and I swallowed hard.

It was River…

Chapter Three

"What are you doing here?" I said through gritted teeth. "I told you never to seek me out ever again." My anger coursed through my body like a shot of adrenaline. "You promised never to see me." The last word came out softer than I hoped, and I swallowed hard, not trusting my voice to speak again.

Luna jumped up and down, her tail wagging, and her tongue hanging out of her mouth when she saw me. I couldn't ignore this sweet girl. This fight was between me and her owner. I crouched down and scratched behind the Mexican Mutt's ears.

River sighed heavily. "Your father needs you," he whispered.

I glared up at him, but he averted his eyes. It didn't help to show him how angry I was after our breakup if he wasn't paying me any attention. I continued scratching behind Luna's ears while she licked me, then I stood up.

Mom and Ralph climbed into the car, giving us privacy; Ralph switched on his radio, blaring country music. While

Mom tried hard to be busy, but I knew she was watching us out of the corner of her eye and most likely going into protective-Mommy-mode.

River's eyes flitted to mine; those amber-brown colored eyes held nothing but pain and sadness. The weight of his emotions was clear on his face. There was much we needed to discuss, but I couldn't do that now. I may never be ready to talk about what would never be.

My anger seeped out of my pores as we stared at each other knowingly. His sad expression matching my own. He was just as heartbroken as I was. We had separated over a year ago, but the heartache was still raw, like it had happened yesterday. And it wasn't just me. He felt the same way.

I'd been working with my father, Victor, in the Underworld until I couldn't anymore. He kept on giving bad guys free passes. These men hurt innocent humans and supernaturals alike without a care in the world because my father would always be there for them. I took it upon myself to go after these bad guys, but no matter how many I killed, more replaced them. My father won in the end when he got contracts for their souls long before he was supposed to, and he kept on getting new souls. It was never ending, and I couldn't continue any longer.

River, on the other hand, could never leave my father's side until his contract was up. He was the one soul I could never help. My father would never give up his best soul; River, no matter how hard I tried, or how much I begged. My father never relented.

I swallowed the emotional lump in my throat and wanted to understand why he was here. "Why does he want me? I told him——"

"He's in trouble," River said, interrupting me. He held

up a hand to shush me, then reached out for me. I didn't want him touching me. I couldn't. Not so soon. I stepped backward. "Please Scout," he said my name with so much emotion the back of my throat ached.

"What did he do this time, or is it like that awful game he made us play and he isn't really in trouble?" My anger had returned, and I felt better. My small black wings flared to life and stretched out behind me. I calmed down and thought hard about hiding them again.

There were things I had to do to gain my much larger wings, but I didn't feel like harming anyone, even though I wanted my fully developed wings. Sometimes being the daughter of a devil didn't sit well with me.

"You need to come home with me." He reached for my hand.

I stepped farther away. "No," I said, shaking my head. "I never want to return. He has demons to help him. Start there."

River shook his head and sank his hands into his deep pockets. "You don't understand, your father is… uh, he isn't who he used to be."

"Your words are cryptic. What do you mean?" I sounded angry again.

He shook his head slowly, his eyes never leaving mine. "Not here. You're too exposed, and I'm being vague on purpose. It's to save both of your lives," he said gravely, making my arms pebble.

I rubbed my arms and stepped closer. "I don't like this."

"Me neither. But you must come with me. It's not something I can say. I need to show you."

My eyes flitted to Mom, who remained in Ralph's car. She stared at me and shrugged as the lines between her eyes deepened.

"Give me a second," I said and approached Ralph's car. Mom wouldn't be pleased if I left without speaking with her first. She lowered her window, and some cheesy song assaulted my ears. She switched off the radio.

"I need to go with River," I said, thumbing over my shoulder. "Something is up with Dad."

"Do you need me to come with?"

"No, I should be ok."

"And you trust him?" she asked, narrowing her eyes at River.

I glanced over my shoulder at River and deep in my heart, I once trusted him with my soul. I hated him at the moment, but I still trusted him. "Yeah," I said, turning back to Mom. "I shouldn't be long." I slapped the car. "I should be home by dinnertime."

"Ok, call me if you need my help." Mom patted my hand and smiled lovingly. "And if you need Zenon, he should be back this afternoon. I'm sure he'd love to help."

"Thanks, Mom."

"Love you."

"Love you, too." I kissed her cheek and approached River.

Chapter Four

River held out his hand. I glared at his large open palm, reminding me of all the times we had held hands. How the warmth of his body had warmed mine like we were meant for each other at soul level. We had been apart for over a year, yet my feelings for him hadn't changed in all this time, and I hated myself for not letting him go.

"I know you can get there yourself, but let me take you to him," he whispered tenderly. His eyes searching mine.

The tension in my shoulders eased. Whatever had happened to Father had nothing to do with River and me. I needed to stop taking it personally and should just take his hand. I relaxed once I resigned to that thought and grabbed his hand.

A warm wind caressed my face as darkness surrounded us. Before, when I teleported with my father, darkness would surround us, wind would whip my face as we moved through space and time, and then he'd teleport us to the Underworld. But with River, his raging flames engulfed us without burning me to a crisp, and we landed in the Eternal

15

Fire in Father's living room with a delicate landing and a soft ping ringing in my ears.

I wanted to panic as the Eternal Fire burned around us. The flames licked against the sides of the fireplace and against the fire-bubble River had created around us. I knew River's flames would protect me and for a second time within five minutes I relaxed and gave in to trusting him. The Eternal Fire wouldn't hurt me if I continued holding River's hand, but the moment I let go, I'd join the rest of the tortured souls in Dad's fireplace.

Luna bolted out of the fireplace first and waited patiently for her owner. River exited next, helping me out, and then let me go. The air popped as if a silky film had surrounded me and I exhaled hot air. My lungs burned as if I'd eaten some of his angry flames. I coughed into my hand as I slowly turned around.

It was the same old living room I'd seen every day for a few years until last year. It had no smell, but the air was fresh. There were no plants or windows, just dim, gargoyle-head torches adorning the walls, which brightened each room.

The gargoyle heads on the walls moved their eyes, following me as I walked around the room. The monster heads were in grotesque stages of near creation; as if the creator had forgotten an important step for each. The one closest to me had a chain through its nose that came out of its empty left eye socket. The chain snaked up the wall, connecting it to the next lamp; this next gargoyle's chain was through its head. In each gargoyle's head, the light shone through their open mouths and eye sockets, screaming in silent torment.

I glanced at my watch and just like last time, the hour hand moved quicker than the seconds while the seconds hand moved at triple the speed. The longer I stared at my watch, the more hypnotized I became. Time was different here, if at all, and one never aged. It amazed me that my watch still worked when I arrived back home. With the hour and second hands moving at odd speeds, one would think the watch would explode.

In one corner was the marble Fountain of Souls with its endless torment of rippling moans and screams. This was part of everyone's journey after they died. Once the ferryman collected a soul, they'd enter the Fountain of Souls before being placed in their rightful area. Where that area was up to them, what they did to others, and what my father felt like doing to their souls. No one was safe here. Not even me.

The same portraits hung on the walls; especially that of my grandfather. His painting reflected his true devil self: a tall creature with crimson eyes, skin the color of blood, and angry horns protruding out the side of his fore-head. He was scary to look at and it was worse in real life. But I knew for a fact that my grandfather was staying at a hotel with many young human females by his side. He enjoyed living as an old man with his white hair flowing over his shoulders because, according to him, *'chicks dig it'*. Apparently, he came across as a vulnerable yet dominant human. I cringed at the thought of someone as old as him doing anything naughty. He sent me postcards at least every six months, letting me know what shenanigans he was up to.

A strange feeling made my skin crawl, but it wasn't River who watched me walk around the room. There was something in the air that made my skin tingle and all the hairs on my body stood up. My fingers danced across the table where food would wait for everyone when Dad hosted

Monster Parties. Now it was empty save for a bowl of rotten fruit, and a worm eating its way through everything.

That eerie feeling thumped against me again like a punch to the face, forcing me to glance in the darkest far corner. There, sitting in the shadows, was a figure covered by dark gray-blue feathers with a hazy-gray-purple hue surrounding him.

My heart thundered in my ears as I slowly approached.

I'd been in this room for what felt like five minutes, and I never noticed him before. Until now. My ears zinged, and a blast of wind hit me in the face before I reached him. River grabbed my shoulders, pulling me back, and shaking his head.

The tall dark angel of death stood up and extended his wings, but they didn't open all the way; instead, they hung limply like water weighed them down. He stretched his shoulders back, trying to make his form larger, but he shrunk an inch before my eyes.

I knew this form to be my father, yet he was different. There was something strange about his demeanor that I couldn't comprehend. Whatever had happened to him, scared me. This being was not the father I knew and loathed. This being was sad looking that bordered on depressing.

"What—" I swallowed hard. "What happened?" I finally said.

"There was an accident," River said, pulling me farther away from Dad.

Victor's power pulsated around me; it was a low hum of pulsing electricity that was nowhere near the power I'd felt before. That power that belonged to Victor could unleash havoc upon the world. Yet, whoever this creature was, whatever Victor was, had changed beyond comprehension, and his power was nothing more than a sizzling flame about to wink out.

Victor was a deity of the dead. It explained where I got my special kind of relationship with the dead from. And it explained why I sensed so many dead souls near him; it wasn't a zombie feeling, but more ghostly—souls—like a dark fog swirling around his aura and mine.

Victor's black armor usually reflected light, giving it a metallic shine, and solid to the touch. It covered his entire body, leaving his face and hands open. But now as I stared wide-eyed at him; his dark feathers were gray, and his armor had lost its shine.

I glanced down at my armor and there was still some shine to it; not as much as I had. I gave him a questioning look.

"I need your help," Victor said, barely above a whisper. He coughed into his fist, and it sounded like it hurt. He winced as he cleared his throat.

"What happened?" I asked again, stepping closer. When River reached for me, I waved him away. Victor was my father. He wouldn't hurt me.

Victor's eyes glowed crimson, reminding me of thirsty vampires I staked when they got too close. I reached for my weapon I kept in a sheath on my belt; a witch had charmed it, and I would use it against him to protect myself.

"Not too close..." Victor cleared his throat again. "I don't know... I may hurt you." His eyes flitted to River behind me. "I'm hungry, yet I cannot eat." His words came out sounding like a growl, and I knew I couldn't trust him, not when he was like this.

I stepped backward, so that I had Victor and River in my peripheral vision. I didn't notice before, but River had a mark across his face; it was faint, but it was there. Victor had hurt River; River was immortal, and he healed quickly, yet there was still a mark.

The lines between my eyes deepened. "What happened to your face?" I said, staring at River.

"You need to retrieve a mask," Victor said, drawing my attention and sitting back down with shaky legs. He landed hard when he lost his grip and moaned in pain.

"How can you feel pain? You shouldn't be feeling anything."

Victor leaned back and stared up at me, his face gaunt and pale. "Mortal..." he said. "I'm mortal and dying. That mask," he pointed at a leather book close to me, "I need that mask to return my powers, or I will die."

"This isn't some prank like last time to help me level up my own powers, is it?" I asked, remembering how I had to complete three tasks to get partial powers and my tiny wings; that were growing slowly.

Victor shook his head and that, too, looked like it hurt. "No game. Real. No time left. Go now or I'll die."

I was silent for a moment as I thought about what was going on. I stared at Victor, who sat there in so much pain, reminding me of a patient with a terminal illness. This was really happening. Somehow my father had gotten hurt... badly; or rather, someone had slipped through his evil defenses and removed his powers from him with a mask. I'd never heard of such an item; it was probably an ancient artifact or something. If this was true, I had to get help, but I wasn't sure how much time we had and what would happen if I didn't get it in time.

"How long does he have?"

"In the real world, we have about a day, maximum two," River said solemnly.

"That all?" I asked sarcastically.

River nodded.

Victor had fallen silent. His breathing was raspy. His feathers whitened along with white streaks appearing in his black hair. A sadness washed over me as I watched parts of his hair turn white, but I was more shocked that someone got it right to do this to him.

"Have you gone through the book?" I asked River and reached for the book Victor had pointed at. "Have you seen this mask?"

"No," he said, shaking his head. "Victor wanted me to fetch you immediately."

"And that?" I pointed at the mark on his face.

"We fought. He thought I was trying to kill him. I think he was delirious because he mumbled words I'd never heard before."

I exhaled frustratingly. "Fine, let's see what this mask looks like."

Chapter Five

Victor's breathing became raspy as he struggled to take in air. He was a supernatural being, and it took a lot to kill him, yet now he was gravely frail. I felt bad for him. Every time he breathed, he winced as if that was too much for his body to handle. I couldn't do anything to ease his pain, but I would find the mask for him.

"He needs to at least recover in comfort," I said, approaching Victor carefully. A strange smell wafted in the air.

"What do you propose?" River asked beside me.

"He has a bedroom?"

"Yeah."

"Let's carry him there. At least he can be on his comfortable bed while we're away."

River nodded. "Sure," then turned to Victor, "my Lord." River waited for Victor to look up at him. River crouched and whispered, "We need to take you to your room, where it's comfortable. Now brace yourself. We need to pick you up."

"Help me stand," Victor said, holding out his hands. "I can try to walk."

We did as he asked and helped him to stand. His eyes continued glowing red, and his fangs elongated. He sniffed the air hungrily. I held onto his waist, and he dropped an arm around my shoulders and the other around River.

"If he's human, how come he still has fangs?" I asked, and we slowly walked with him through the lounge and down the corridor toward his bedroom.

"I don't know," River said. "I can only guess that it's slowly making him more human. And whatever is going on inside his body is hurting him."

I sniffed the air and the stench of old, dirty soup I'd smelled earlier clung to me. I said nothing, but guessed it was Dad who desperately needed a bath.

We slowly traversed down the corridor, passing the room with the occupant who scared me the first time I was here. Then we passed the bathroom and then my old room, and headed for the end of the hallway. I was about to ask where it was when a door appeared up ahead, as if sensing Victor. The elegantly carved wood depicted various flowers and trees with fruit. River opened the door, and the carvings changed. The fruit slowly becoming rotten and falling to the ground.

"We're almost there," River said out of breath.

Victor was heavy, but not that heavy; I wasn't out of breath yet, but River was. We turned Victor around and helped him sit on the bed. He scooted to the middle of the bed and laid down, closing his eyes.

"Come, let him rest," River said, pulling me away.

Victor seemed so beyond reach, almost a distant memory, as I watched his ragged breathing and his skin becoming paler. I had to help him before he had his last breath. I glanced at River, who stared back at me knowingly.

River and I walked back to the living room in silence. I exhaled a weary breath as we sat on the large sofa in the Underworld to review the book that had information on the mask.

We paged through the book quietly, with only the sound of our shallow breathing breaking the silence. I read the heading of each page before turning it, only to find the next page had nothing on masks. The surrounding air chilled my bones, and I closed my jacket. My mind kept wandering to Victor and how awful he looked and that I couldn't believe such an awful artifact existed. Slowly, the little bit of energy I had was dwindling. Tears welled in my eyes, but I faked a yawn so that I could wipe my eyes dry without alerting River. I was sad, but I didn't feel like talking about it.

"Wait," River said, jumping up and wearing a smile. "The atmosphere is depressing. There's no way we can concentrate on anything if we're like this. How about I make us some tea; not the murky gunk the Underworld Chef makes."

"Yeah, you're right. Let's drink tea," I said, smiling. River was right; I'd been turning pages in that old book but seeing none of them. I couldn't concentrate because all I saw was my gaunt-looking father, who had one leg in the grave and one in the Underworld. Giggling at the thought, I glanced around to make sure nobody had witnessed my smile, and immediately felt guilty.

I sighed as I wondered if my dad died who would welcome him to the Underworld since he was already here. Then I thought about my father's soul and if he even had one. He had to have one. All supernaturals had. My thoughts crashed one into the other, making my head and heart hurt.

"Here," River said, holding a cup of strong tea near my nose. It had full cream milk and two sugars, like I always drank it.

"Thank you," I said, smiling and taking the cup from his hands.

He sat beside me. I sat with my legs crossed on the couch and the large leather book propped on my legs. We sipped from our cups as I paged through the book, ignoring the heat from his body beat against mine.

I eventually found the page Victor had alluded to that featured information on a mask that was once thought lost. They had buried it inside the sarcophagus of a pharaoh years ago. When someone wore the mask, it turned a normal human immortal and gave them a power unique to that individual. But, if an immortal wore the mask, it removed their power, making them human, sickly and they would ultimately die. Which explained why Victor was dying.

I rubbed my face and finished my tea. "Do you know who found the mask and used it on Victor?"

River shook his head in shame. "No, but what bothers me the most I was meant to accompany him, but he sent me on a foolish errand. When I returned, he attacked me. Once I stabilized him and he was almost coherent, he told me to fetch you. Then, only when you found the information on the mask, could I give you this." River handed me an ancient envelope. "He said only you should read it."

I took the envelope from him and opened it;

Professor Alexander Dakin

I turned the piece of paper around, but there was nothing other than one man's name. "I guess we need to find him." Standing up, I grabbed Father's leather satchel and placed the book inside, along with the envelope. "The sooner we get to him, the better. Now, how do we find him?"

"Google?"

Chapter Six

There was only one Professor Alexander Dakin. Ever. In the whole wide world. He lived in Egypt and taught students about Ancient Egypt. It relieved me that there was only one person with that name, therefore it wasn't necessary to visit more than one place; saving us time. We had to get to him the quickest way possible, and that was by teleporting.

Years ago when I'd completed the tasks as set out by my father, my rite of passage into the family, I mastered one of his powers; teleporting. It was only possible to teleport myself for now, and I no longer experienced any nausea.

"Ready?" River asked, holding out his hand. Luna sat beside him with one paw on his shoe and her long tongue sticking out one side of her toothy jaw.

"I can get there myself," I said, raising my chin.

"I know, but I'd rather we arrive at the same place together instead of at different locations. I don't feel like searching for you first and then for the professor. It's a waste of time," he moaned, arching an eyebrow.

I curled my lips over my teeth as I tried to smile. He was right, and I hated that. "Fine," I grumbled and grabbed his hand, squeezing that much harder. "Let's get this over with."

"I don't know why you're angry. You're the one who left me." He squeezed gently back and closed his eyes. The warmth from his hand reminded me of our good times together, and my heart fluttered inside my chest. "Let's work together for a couple of hours... for your father. Then you can go back to hating me."

I exhaled an irritated breath. He was right. I could work with him for a day or two. We were doing this to save my father. "Fine," I said, glancing at his profile. "Let's do this." I smiled inside—I could do this—and closed my eyes.

Wind smacked my face and my long hair floated as we moved through space and time. Before I could open my mouth to complain we were moving too fast, we landed with a thud on solid ground.

Usually, when I teleported myself, the landings were gentle, but doing it with River now threw me off balance and my face smacked into his chest. It was like my cheek hit a soft brick wall. I let go of his hand and pushed him away from me.

Luna jumped up and down with excitement and barked at a butterfly near her face.

"We haven't done that in a while," River said with a smirk, rubbing the spot where I'd hit him with my face.

I grunted in response and tied my hair in a low ponytail.

"Your hair has grown," he said, reaching for it. "Still as beautiful as ever."

Frowning, I didn't know if he was referring to my hair or me and stepped farther away from him, so he couldn't touch me more than necessary. "I'm growing it." I flicked the ponytail over my shoulder so that it could rest between my shoulder blades. The end of the ponytail almost reached my bum. "Where must we go?" I said, glancing around and desperately wanting to change the subject.

The large university seemed ancient, with its columns, high ceilings, and the smell of ancient dusty books. I wanted to say something when a murder of crows flew overhead; none were my crows though. If I needed my spirit animals, all I had to do was call Jake and the rest would follow. I didn't need them... yet.

River crossed the courtyard without answering me, and I followed closely behind him. We entered the double doors leading us to the lecturers' lounge, but the room was vacant, neat, and tidy. The smell of ancient, dusty books was strongest here, along with the stench of day-old sandwiches.

There were frames with pictures of all the university lecturers on the walls and old books on the tables in the room. Some books were open, as if the teachers were reading when asked to vacate the premises.

"What day is it?" I asked, trying to open the door leading to the staff kitchen.

"It's still Sunday," River said, holding up a newspaper and pointed at the date. "Not much time had passed since you left your mother in Sterling Meadow." Then he pointed at something behind me.

I turned around and on a corkboard stuck with a thumbtack, was an A4 piece of paper with all the lecturer's room numbers printed in small font. I neared and squinted as I traced with my finger until I found the professor's room on the map at the bottom of the page.

"That's where we have to go," I said, beaming as a

flutter of joy flowed through my chest that we were a step closer to finding the mask than before.

The hallways were quiet apart from our footsteps hitting the ceramic tiles. "I know it's Sunday, but aren't universities always open?" I whispered, but my voice still bounced off the walls in stereo. "Usually there are staff members around every day of the week. Why is it so empty?"

River pointed to the right. "Not sure why it's empty, but we need to go that way."

As we turned the corner, a dark green and red blur smashed into us, knocking us into each other, and we crashed to the floor.

"What the hell?" River said, rubbing his forehead. Luna barked and ran after the blurry figure. River jumped up and started after the person, but they were already gone. "Where did he go?"

Luna continued barking until another butterfly sat on her nose, quietening her.

"Ow," I said, rubbing my head. I sat up and watched River saunter back to me. My hands began to sweat, and my heart raced inside my chest. I glanced away and used the wall to climb to my feet.

"He's gone. Whatever he was, he flew out," River said when he reached me and flapped his hands in the air like he was a bird.

Luna ran toward us, her long tongue flapping outside of her mouth. She looked goofy, yet adorable.

"Let's find the professor's office." I turned, still rubbing my head, and quickened my step in that direction.

River and Luna were behind me, but I didn't wait for them to catch up to me. I found the professor's office and stopped in the doorjamb. My fingers dug into the wooden frame while my eyes danced across the messy floor. There were papers strewn everywhere, along with shattered glass. But it was the red liquid seeping in the light-brown carpet near his desk that caught my attention.

I ran inside and fell to my knees on the edge of the widening red liquid. I reached over and felt his pulse near his neck, but there was none. My hand came away with his still warm blood. River handed me a tissue he'd grabbed from the floor, and I wiped my hand clean; but his blood had already stained the creases of my palm.

Luna sniffed around the professor's body and whined.

"I can safely assume that thing that smacked into us did this." I stood and pointed at the deceased as I tried to recall what I had seen before it smashed into us. All I could remember was dark green and red blurs and then River and me connecting heads.

"Uh-huh," River said as he surveyed the room. "My vision is good, but I didn't see it coming," he said, deep in thought. "And it's obvious it was here looking for something." He crouched near a heap on the floor, using his index finger to pick through the mess.

"Maybe the same thing we're here for." The room was a mess, and I didn't know where to start.

"Uh-huh," River said nonchalantly and crossed the disorderly floor to look at the books on the shelves against the wall. "We'll need to get out of here quickly before they think we did this," he said absentmindedly.

I felt the professor's pockets for anything but found nothing. A locket on a chain moved out from under his clothing. I opened it and smiled when I saw a picture of two young boys kicking a ball.

I stood and searched his desk, moving pens and papers out of my way. I lifted ornaments and paperweights to see what they were holding down, but there was nothing of interest. It wasn't as if I was making a mess to an already mess, but I neatened the papers and stacked them to one side.

Then I searched inside the drawers, flipping through booklets, and felt at the top for any secret compartments. If there was one thing I'd learned since working with my mother was that more people had little hideaways for their secret stash. The trick was to find them. When my hand found a button, my heart raced with excitement as I pressed it. Something sounded behind me like cogs moving and a book popped out of the shelves without crashing to the floor. The entire experience reminded me of an adventure movie.

I reached for the book when River's hand joined mine. I smacked his hand away. "Mine," I said with a playful growl. "Go get your own book from a secret compartment."

River chuckled and stood closer. "I wonder what else he has hidden here." He glanced up at the high ceiling and the walls lined with bookshelves.

"Continue looking before others arrive." I opened the book and leafed through the pages. It had diary entries from 1988. I browsed through the diary, reading a few entries mentioning Alec and an institute. The professor felt guilty for leaving him there and not being able to help. Then the entries stopped, and I wanted to understand what the professor meant when he had written he couldn't stop them. Who was he talking about?

Someone coughed behind me, and I froze. River was still beside me and continued rummaging through the book-shelves as if he had heard nothing. "River?" I whispered. "Did you cough?"

"Huh," River said, looking at me with a confused expression. "No."

Slowly, I turned around. A gray figure with his throat slit, no blood, floated above the professor's corpse. The translucent figure pointed at his neck, then at the neck of the corpse on the floor. The locket still lay open on his chest, but the picture of the two boys had changed.

I pushed souls out of bodies, and I saw souls. That was my dominant power. I could also animate corpses by bringing their souls back into their bodies, but I didn't do that often because I didn't like a live offering in which to do it; sacrificing an animal just to bring someone back was dark magic. I wanted nothing to do with it. But when a soul reached out to me, they usually had something to show me; sometimes they could speak, other times they were mute and had to point at certain things to explain what was going on.

I slipped the book inside my satchel and approached the corpse cautiously and crouched down.

"What are you doing?" River asked, but I ignored him.

I stared up at the gray figure floating above my head. He moved backward, pointing at his neck again. I nodded my understanding and picked up the locket, carefully removing it from the professor's neck. The last thing I wanted was an angry soul because I wasn't gentle enough with his head.

River stood beside me, watching intently, and wearing a confused expression. "What are you doing and what do you keep looking at?" When I didn't answer him, I saw in my peripheral vision his nod. "You're communicating with his soul, isn't it?" For some strange and twisted reason, River couldn't always see souls like I could. He could kill a human by snapping his finger, but souls, nope, he only saw them sometimes.

When working a case with Mom, we sometimes needed

information from the recently deceased. That was the only time I could channel my power by returning their soul to their body, animating the corpse, and without a sacrifice. But they had to have died within the last thirty minutes of their death or it wouldn't work; unless I sacrificed an animal. But today I didn't feel like bringing the professor back to life, since his soul was already helping us.

I stared at the picture in the locket; it had changed, showing two older boys fighting. "Is this you?" I asked the gray figure. He nodded and started fading. "Is there anything else you want to show me?" I asked quickly, standing up. "Do you know who did this to you?" I pointed at the professor.

The figure shook its head, then pointed at the window the moment sirens wailed outside as police vans pulled up, their blue and red lights a warning.

"We have to go," I said, turning back toward the figure. "Is there another way out of here?"

The figure slowly started fading, but before it disappeared completely, it pointed toward the far corner of the room, near the door.

"That way," I said confidently, pointing and heading that way.

As I passed the figure I whistled that specific tune and the ferryman appeared. The ghostly figure floated into the boat and they sailed away peacefully. And something told me his soul would be well looked after.

When the sound of someone yelling and approaching footsteps neared, I snapped out of it and headed for the corner the soul had pointed at.

River was already there, feeling the sides of the bookcase. He flicked something, and the bookcase moved away from the wall. "Bingo," he said and entered with Luna hot on his heels.

When the shouting and footsteps outside became louder. I grabbed the door, stepping through the opening, and closed the bookcase behind me as they others burst through the professor's door.

Chapter Seven

"Where are we?" I whispered as I felt the damp walls and carefully descended the dark steps.

"I don't care, just as long as it gets us out of here safely." River tripped and tumbled down the stairs. He burst into a ball of angry flames, illuminating the stairwell.

"Why didn't you do that earlier?" I asked playfully. "Then maybe you wouldn't have fallen."

"It's not as if I can hurt myself." River stood up, dusted his clothing, and pulled spiderwebs off his shoulder. His skeleton was aflame, and I marveled at the fact that his clothing never burned off his body.

"Can you stay like that until we're out of here?"

"Yeah, sure," he grumbled. "It reminds me of all those games we played for your father and all our little adventures." He smirked as best he could with his skeleton head.

"Yep," I said sadly, but now wasn't the time to go down memory lane regarding our relationship. "Now let's see where this takes us."

We continued down the stairs in silence, and River

stayed in his state of flames. Water continued dripping down the sides of the curved wall as we followed the spiral staircase down.

"I never asked this before, but do your flames come from the Eternal Flame in the Underworld?"

River stopped and stared up at me; the flaming orbs where his eyes were meant to be stared at me, through me, as if conjuring the answer to appear before me.

"Probably," he said, thinking about the question. "I've never asked Victor, but I guess so." He shrugged and the flames on his shoulders flared to life, licking the wall behind him. "I think everything is connected to the Underworld in some way."

"I think so too. Look," I said, pointing at the light up ahead. "It seems we have a way out. Extinguish your flames before you scare a poor human walking past."

As River neared the exit, he exhaled loudly and the fire abruptly disappeared, as if he absorbed every hot flame. He twisted the door handle and opened it.

The bright light of the sun burned my eyes, forcing me to cover my face with my left hand, and followed River outside. Sirens continued wailing in the distance. It relieved me the secret exit led us to the outskirts of the university perimeter near a storm drain. The high walls surrounding the university stood before us like gate keepers; each face-brick a similar sandy color with individual patterns on. The wall looked like it moved, reminding me of slithering snakes.

I shuddered. Everything about this university reminded me of that game Father played with me; it's how I got my wings. Just thinking about my black wings and they appeared. I rarely used them when I worked with Mom; it scared the humans and the supernaturals always wanted to touch them. I rounded my shoulders, and the wings disappeared.

"This way," River said, pulling me out of my thoughts.

"Where are we going?" I asked, my feet sinking into the soft sand. "There's nothing out here but sand." The university was on the outskirts of the city where the Egyptian sand blended with concrete and civilization. If we went the other way, we had to pass the police, and that was a bad idea.

"I know, but we don't want to go in the other direction. At least this way we have space to escape."

"Wait," I said, grabbing his jacket to stop him. "Look," I said, opening the locket. The picture of the two boys had changed. It was now of a man wearing a white gown with his name sewn on, and underneath was the name of the institution. I pitied him as he rocked back and forth, reminding me of a movie.

"Do you want to go to his brother?"

"Why not? We have nothing else to go on. And besides, he might have more information for us. And look," I pointed at the name, "Alec Dakin, Lake Hills Institute." I grinned. All the pieces of the puzzle just fell in our laps.

River nodded, but unconvincingly.

"What's wrong?" I asked, narrowing my eyes.

He sighed audibly, not looking me in the eye.

"What is it? If you don't want to go here, where do you want to go?"

River pulled a newspaper clipping from his jacket pocket.

"How do your flames not burn everything to ashes?"

"Like I said years ago, things will only burn if I want them to."

"And what is that, anyway?" I said, snatching the clipping from his fingertips. "Where did you get this?"

"It was near the professor's body. It looked important."

I took a moment to look at the article. "You're right. This could answer all our questions."

"I know," he said, grinning.

River held out his hand, and I begrudgingly took it. Luna jumped up against his leg and he rubbed her side, calming her. She twirled around and sat on his shoe. "Ready?" he said, closing his eyes. I nodded, and we teleported to the tomb where they'd discovered the mask.

Chapter Eight

We landed in a sandstorm, and immediately fell to our knees to avoid a branch of the only tree standing beside an ancient structure crashing into us. The branch whooshed over our heads as sand pelted our skin. To be sandblasted was not fun, and I huddled into my jacket.

I squeezed my eyes shut, waiting for the worst to blow over. When the wind died down, I glanced at our surroundings. I slung my satchel over my head, so it sat snuggly across my chest and patted the journal I'd taken from the professor's office; it was secure, and the locket was in one pocket of the satchel.

The wind picked up a notch again, forcing me to clutch the strap tighter against my chest with one hand and my jacket with the other. Raising my elbow, I tried to protect my face, but sand kept smacking me where it hurt.

"Here," River said, grabbing my arm.

We took cover inside the main entrance of the tomb to catch our breaths. I groaned inwardly at the various hieroglyphics on the walls, the dark atmosphere of the tomb, and the markings on the stone at our feet. I imagined the troubles that lay ahead of us once we entered the main building.

"Are you ready?"

"Not really," I said, turning around. "We know nothing about this place." I pointed at a hieroglyphic where a man's head was being chopped off at an altar. "What if there's a curse laid upon us when entering?"

"We won't know until we enter." River pointed at another entrance inside.

"Yeah, sure, but by then it will be too late," I groaned, staring at a sun with serpents and another of a man holding a mask. At least we were in the right place if they had originally buried the mask here.

"Come," River said, calling me over. "I'll go first."

"Good. They can attack you first." I just wanted to get this over and done with. As much as I hated my father, I didn't want him to suffer or die, and the sooner I got home to my safe room and Netflix, the better.

"Do you talk to your father at all?" River asked, pushing the wooden door open and entering first like he promised. He checked left, then right, and entered when no ghost or mummy attacked him.

"No," I said, following him. "He knows I hate what he does—"

"Collect souls?"

"Not only that, but how he does it and the fact that the bad guys keep doing what makes them bad."

"He gets them in the end—"

"I know," I raised my hands, "you don't have to tell me. My father gets the bad guys in the end, but it's the innocent victims they leave behind that I'm more concerned about."

"They aren't all that innocent. There's a reason they are there—"

"Okay, enough. I don't want to debate this with you," I groaned, wiping spider webs off my shoulder and out of my face. "Can you help? We need to see the tomb where they took the picture." I sounded as grumpy as I felt, and sighed audibly.

"You know I can help." River held out his hand, and it caught flame; then he wiggled his fire-tip-phalanges.

"Show-off," I grumbled and followed his light down an internal passage and into a larger tomb. It felt like a scene out of Indiana Jones and I wished I had learned how to use a braided kangaroo leather whip. At least that way I could smack River on his bum and still have time to get away before he caught me. I smiled at the thought, then quickly squashed it.

"Is it just me or does it look like nobody has been here... in years," River said, crouching near the closed sarcophagus.

The tomb housed the pharaoh who had discovered the mask; well, that's what I read in the newspaper article. When the supernaturals had found out someone had created such a mask, they didn't want to touch it for fear of losing their power. They placed the mask inside a container and forced the pharaoh to place it in his sarcophagus with him as a punishment for finding the artifact. Then they buried the tomb, hiding it, but over time, sand had eroded away, opening the tomb for discovery.

"According to the newspaper, they found the mask two weeks ago. How come this chamber looks undisturbed?" River held up the newspaper article. "I wonder if they staged this picture."

The photo showed four people standing near the tomb with the professor in front of the same sarcophagus we stood near now, except in the photo it was open. Yet everything about the chamber now was undisturbed.

"This looks like the same place, yet it's different." I scrunched my face in confusion. "This chamber hasn't seen people in years. The last time anyone was in here was when they buried him." I raised my hand to my nose and sneezed. "Even the dust is old." Cobwebs clung to the corners. Beetles scuttled across the floor. While other unknown insects stood against the walls staring at us.

River walked around the tomb with his fiery hands in the air, looking at the various hieroglyphics. "It looks exactly like the newspaper picture. Anyway, let's see inside," he said, pointing at the sarcophagus and approached carefully.

Luna stood beside him, waiting patiently.

He didn't wait for my help and pushed the heavy slab to the side. Dust danced in the surrounding air, and he waved his flaming hand in front of his face.

"No mask here," he said, reaching inside.

I looked inside to make sure he was telling the truth and it was just the dead pharaoh. They had tightly wrapped his body in linen. Sand over the years had made its way inside, while broken cobwebs had fixed to the corners.

I leaned against the sarcophagus, placing my hands on the edge, and felt the cold stone beneath my fingertips. My half-brother Zenon would love to see this. He was interested in all things Egyptian, and the various artifacts discovered. If he were here, he'd be able to assist us quicker. He could also read the hieroglyphics for us.

I glanced up at River, who was already staring at me. "What?"

"You think your brother could help?" His eyes narrowed. "Is that what you're thinking?"

"Yeah," I couldn't help the grin stretching my face, "he loves this stuff. Don't you think he could assist us?"

"I don't care who helps, just as long as we save Victor. He can't die." The lines between his eyes deepened, and the recently made wound by Victor was slowly fading, but River was still a bit on the pale side.

I stared at River as I considered his words. It was then that I realized that if Victor died, the possibility of River going down with him was that much greater. My father had tied River to him in more ways than I could imagine. And as much as River and I fought, I didn't want to see him get hurt. I loved him once and although we spoke little, I still wanted the best for him.

Something flickered in his eyes akin to recognition and I knew then I didn't have to say anything; we both knew how his life would end if Victor didn't make it.

"I'm going to call him."

Chapter Nine

I just got off the phone with Mom when Zenon appeared at the foot of the structure near the same tree as we had, but without the sandblasting. He landed softly on the sand like a dangerous angel and casually traversed the soft sand. He moved so swiftly I thought he was floating above the sand.

My half-brother had two fathers, who were brothers; Sebastian and Léon. My mother loved both men and was still in a relationship with both. She fell pregnant with Zenon when I was sixteen. I was twenty-three now and my brother was twenty-eight and would remain so until someone killed him; on the odd occasion, I vowed to end his life, but we always ended our argument with a hug. We were an all-talk-and-no-action kind of family.

From the moment Zenon was born, he had aged quickly. The first year of his life, he had developed similar characteristics to Sebastian; they're both were-leopards and vampires. And although Léon was the Master Vampire of Sterling Meadow, he didn't turn into anything furry once a month like Sebastian and Zenon.

We were a complicated family, but we loved each other and would protect each other to the nth degree. I had struggled with my mom's relationships at first, but the two brothers had grown on me and I loved them like fathers; especially after I realized my real father wasn't as great as I thought he would be.

I watched Zenon traverse the stairs, and my smile matched his. When he looked up at me, his yellow/golden eyes, with a green sliver in each iris, twinkled in the sunlight. This was another way of knowing who Zenon's true father was; the eyes. Sebastian's eye color was green, with a golden sliver through each iris. Their eye colors were strikingly beautiful, making them very handsome men. Zenon was much taller than River and me and I had to crane my neck up to look at him.

"Little sister," Zenon said, bringing me in for a hug. "It's been like what, two days since I last saw you. What are you doing here?" he asked, glancing around and dusting sand off his shoulders.

I smacked his chest. "I'm not little. Anyway, we need your help," I said, smiling.

Zenon nodded in River's direction as a way of greeting. They never got along, but they tolerated each other for my sake. I sighed silently.

"So what's the dealio with him?" Zenon jerked his chin in River's direction. "I thought you two weren't together anymore." Anger slipped out of Zenon like a waterfall, reminding me of Mom and her anger bursts.

"Easy there, he's helping me." I rubbed my tired eyes. "As I explained when I phoned, Victor is in grave danger and we need to find an artifact thought lost. They used the artifact on Victor and if we find it and use it on him again, we hope it will reverse any damage done to him. We first went to the professor, but found his body instead. Then we came here after River found the newspaper article," I rambled, taking my first breath since I started explaining to Zenon, again. "I was thinking, since you know a lot about these things, perhaps you can help us quicker," I said at a normal pace. "Maybe the pretty pictures on the walls can help us." I pointed at the hieroglyphics.

Zenon narrowed his eyes at River while I spoke. When I was done, he held his hands behind his back, reminding me of Léon, and walked around River, then entered the structure. "Well, come on, let's see what's going on."

I gave Zenon more information about what we were seeking, and he listened carefully. He traversed around the tomb and peeked inside the sarcophagus. When I finished, he stopped and stared at me, his twinkling yellow/golden eyes smiling.

"You do realize that when we find this mask, none of us may touch it. And if a human touches it, they will become the monster that lives deep within." He shook his head as if expelling an idea. "This artifact is an abomination, and we should destroy it."

"It's the only thing that can save Victor," I said with pleading eyes. "We can't destroy it."

"Do you think I care about him?" Zenon said, his voice raised. "He's done nothing but hurt our mother, almost destroyed you, and not to mention all the innocent lives he ruins collecting souls." He was shouting now. The veins in his neck bulged and his cheeks glowed red.

I raised my hands. "Not one to upset you, but you're preaching to the choir. I get it. I agree, and I hate what my father does for a living. There are days I hate him for what he is. Then I hate the fact that I can see the dead and can hurt those around me with the palms of my hands," I raised my hands, and stared at my palms, "and I'm yet to discover all I can do and believe me when I say I get it…" My shoulders sagged as I exhaled. "I get it," I said softer. "But he's still my father." My voice broke at the thought of losing another father. I'd lost Mason, the man who had raised and protected me my entire life, and now I was on the verge of losing another one. I had Sebastian and Léon, but they were different.

Zenon pulled me into an embrace, resting his chin on my head, and patted my shoulder. "It's okay, sister, we'll sort something out."

I understood what Zenon was getting at. We would destroy ourselves if we touched that mask, and I didn't know how we could solve the problem.

"I agree with your assumption," Zenon said, letting go and standing back. "No one has disturbed this tomb in years, and I doubt they took that picture here." He took the newspaper clipping out of River's hands and stared at it. "And according to this, they took it two weeks ago." He shook his head, pointing at the date on the clipping. "It's staged. Either they are lying about discovering the mask, or they lied to your father and there's something else we need to look for."

Zenon read the hieroglyphics on the walls and on the sides of the sarcophagus. "The rituals written on the walls bind the mask to the tomb with time," he said, deep in thought. "I don't understand that. Maybe it's my interpretation of the symbols. I do know that time is an important factor here." He fell silent for a moment as he looked at the symbols again, his hand trailing across the ridges. "But it's not only the mask, there's something about this tomb itself." He shook his head as if dispelling his thoughts. "If they could release the mask from here, someone powerful had to do it."

"The mask isn't here," I said. "What do we do now?"

Zenon pointed at my hand. "What about the locket? The brothers. One is already dead, let's go visit the other one. Maybe he has more information for us."

Chapter Ten

River held out his hand. Luna barked, wanting to come with. "Stay," he said, pointing to a corner of the tomb. Luna yelped and walked to the corner with her tail between her legs.

"Why don't you want her to come with?" I asked, holding his hand.

"I don't need her at the moment and think it's better if she stays here for now. If I need her, I'll call her. She can get to me on her own."

Luna turned around in a circle, finding the right spot and settled down. With her head on her front paws, her big brown pleading eyes stared longingly at us.

I grabbed Zenon's hand so that we could teleport and arrive at the institute together. I loved teleporting with Zenon. He moved through space and time much faster than anyone else. I knew little about all the powers he wielded—he wasn't one for boasting about what he could do—and based on his quick teleporting; he was formidable.

When I opened my eyes, we stood outside the gates of

Lake Hills Institute. I cocked my head to the side and frowned. "Why does this place feel familiar?" I asked, letting go of their hands and traversed down the steps to the front gate.

I'd never been here before, yet it felt like déjà vu. I stared up at the three and a half floors; the half was the attic at the top with clean crescent windows. They painted the walls a sterile white with gray-colored window frames. The lawn out front was in pristine condition, with neatly trimmed hedges.

"This doesn't exactly scream asylum, does it?" Zenon mumbled beside me. He curled his top lip over his fangs as he tasted the air. Sometimes he was all animal.

"You'll fit right in," I said, teasing.

"Ha," he said with one side of his mouth curved upward.

"It's a hospital for the special, I think." When I said special, I used air quotes.

"Crazy, you mean."

I slapped his shoulder. "You'd definitely fit in then."

"Let's check it out," Zenon said, walking ahead of me.

I flinched when a chime sounded from somewhere inside the building. Zenon stopped dead on the last step and glanced over his shoulder with raised eyebrows.

River passed us and yanked on the rope near the door, ringing the antique bell. It clanked, hurting my ears.

A nurse appeared on the other side of the locked gate, wearing a smile and a sterile white uniform from the sixties with a nursing cap to complete the look. "May I help you?" she asked, grabbing hold of the rope to stop it from hitting the bell.

Zenon cleared his throat and glanced at me again.

I coughed into my hand and pushed past the men. "Hi,

my name is Scout, and I was wondering if we could speak with someone who runs this place. We would like to know if you have an Alec Dakin here and if so, can we see him?" I pulled out the locket and showed her the picture of the professor's brother wearing a white gown. He continued rocking back and forth in the moving picture. I pointed at his name and the name of the institution sewn into his uniform.

"Oh, dear me," the nurse said, opening the gate. "Come inside. You'll need to speak with Isaac Hilling first."

As we entered the institute, on the right-hand side of the entrance next to the front door hung a plaque with a large picture frame. It read that the school had opened in 1889 and housed 'talented' children. I wasn't sure if they meant the kids had a disability or they were supernatural.

They had pictures of about twenty staff members framing the photo. They all wore white; comprising nurses, orderlies, and the man in the middle who opened the place —Curtis Hilling. Underneath the frame hung more plaques stating which of the Hilling sons had taken over and from which year. Arthur took over from his father in 1901, and Isaac currently managed the institute from 1946.

I frowned, wondering who had managed the institute now in 2023. I glanced at River, who shrugged, and Zenon shook his head. It seemed we were all thinking the same thing.

"This building has been around for quite a while," I said, pointing at the frames as I passed the nurse.

She nodded and smiled, and as she blinked, her nicti-tating membrane shifted into view; a transparent third eyelid moving across each eye, reminding me of a crocodile or lizard. I swallowed hard. I'd never come across cold-blooded shifters before and grabbed Zenon's hand, forcing him to stay beside me. He squeezed my hand back, noticing the same thing. It relieved me that Zenon was here, limiting my interaction with River. Although I was glad he was with, the wounds were still fresh and the less I was near him, the better for me.

"Yes," the nurse said, "we take in abandoned children and allow them to thrive as they are destined to. They either leave the institute once able to or we continue to provide them with the safety of remaining here until adulthood. Some have even died of old age here." Her eyes flitted to a section beyond the border of the house, and I surmised it was their graveyard.

"Do you take in any child or only supernatural children?" I asked carefully and stepped backward... in case she wanted to lunge at us.

The nurse grinned, and it reached her eyes. Her pointy teeth stuck out from under her top lip. "Like you and everyone here, they're supernatural." She entered the building first, her heels clicking against the hard floor. "This way."

We followed her through the large hallways of the institute, the security gate slamming closed behind us. A nervousness shot up my spine that we might be stuck in here, but I knew that not to be true, we could teleport our way out.

The nurse led us down a long hallway and stopped outside an office with a door plaque that read Isaac Hilling. She entered, whispering something to him, then when she came back out, she nodded and said, "He will see you now." She bowed her head slightly and promptly left like she was the only one who heard a phone ringing somewhere in the distance.

"Hi, please come in. I understand you wish to see one

of our patients?" Isaac said, standing up from behind his desk with his hand outstretched. He too blinked, and the third eyelid closed and opened again. His forked tongue slithered out of his mouth, then quickly shifted into a human tongue. I suspected he was tasting the air; perhaps tasting how dangerous we were or whether we were scrumptious enough to eat.

I placed my hands on my hips, caressing the hilt of the knife at my back. I could always use my hands and shove his soul out of his body, but only if I had to.

"Thank you for seeing us, Mr. Hilling," I said, finally shaking his hand. "My name is Scout. This is River, and that's Zenon."

"Please sit and call me Isaac. My dad was Mr. Hilling." He smiled warmly, but there was something about him I didn't like. Whether it was the way he smiled, the scales that appeared, then disappeared, or just his demeanor.

"It's fine. We won't stay long, Isaac." We didn't sit, but stared down at the man. I hoped by outnumbering him he would think twice about eating us.

"Right. My nurse says you want to see Alec Dakin? May I see the picture in the locket to be sure we have the right patient?"

I showed him the picture but kept the locket in my hand. He tried to take it, but I held on. He peered over his gold-rimmed glasses at me when he realized he couldn't take it and stood up again to see it properly. I doubted he needed his glasses to see, since he was a cold-blooded shifter. I was yet to hear of any shifter needing any kind of device to make their lives easier.

I stared at the top of his head as he watched the picture move; the professor's brother rocking backward and forward, backward and forward.

Isaac had brown hair and freckled skin. The back of his neck seemed a little loose as it moved when he did; it was strange, like he wore a mask and the fake skin he wore was too large for him. This was odd, since he was a shapeshifter. He didn't need to wear fake skin or a mask.

Isaac stood straight and cleared his throat. "Alec Dakin came to us two weeks ago. He and his brother had discovered a mask in a sarcophagus in Egypt and he was the unlucky one who picked it up. Apparently, it did something to him. He hasn't said a word since then. And that's the only thing he does all day." He pointed at the locket of Alec rocking backward and forward.

"Do you know if he was a shifter or a supernatural being before he picked up the mask?" I asked, wondering whether Professor Alexander Dakin was one too and didn't know. The professor's throat was slit from ear to ear, and he'd bled out. If he was a shifter or some supernatural being, surely, he would've been able to fight his attacker. Or perhaps he too had held the mask and rendered mortal thereafter. But, if that was the case, why didn't the brothers suffer as violently and quickly as Victor.

I glimpsed at River, who was too busy looking around the office. I was thinking this was way more complicated than I initially thought. It wasn't a straightforward retrieval, but something else.

"We understand he and his brother are supernatural, but it was only the professor who survived the incident with all his wits about him. We still don't know what type of supernatural they were though," Isaac said, moving around his desk and pouring himself a glass of water. "Would you like something to drink?"

"No thank you," I said. "I don't suppose you know whether Alec can speak with us?" I didn't know how the brothers related to Victor's accident, but asking questions would help us understand what happened to the brothers.

Isaac turned to face me with his drink in hand and enjoyed a long sip, his eyes not leaving mine. When the glass was empty, he placed it back onto the tray beside the water jug. "Since his arrival," Isaac said, wiping his mouth dry. "He hasn't said a word. Perhaps you should ask him yourself. Maybe you'll have better luck than I."

Isaac approached the door, and we stepped out of his way. "Follow me," he said, calling us over. "Let's see how he's doing today."

We followed Isaac up the stairs to the second floor. As we passed each open room, I couldn't help but look. There were well-behaved children playing on the floor with old toys while others were sleeping. And in one bedroom, the kids just sat in their chairs and stared out of the window.

Isaac paused in the doorjamb of the last room at the end of the hallway. "You're welcome to stay as long as Alec wants you to stay. He isn't violent or anything like that, but you must be gentle with him. He's a little skittish, if you know what I mean," Isaac said with a compassionate smile. "Good luck." And with his parting greeting, Isaac left us alone with a man who rocked near an open window.

When Isaac was gone, we entered the room.

"Alec?" I said, knocking on the door as I entered. "My name is Scout. Is it all right if we come inside and speak with you?"

Alec's room was sterile with the smell of disinfectants wafting in the air with a copper coin undertone. I wondered if they had hurt him and cleaned him quickly.

Alec stopped rocking and glanced up at us with unshed tears in his eyes. "I'm so glad you've finally arrived."

Chapter Eleven

Shocked down to my core, all I could do was stare at him. Alec stood and opened his shirt, revealing healing wounds from previous incisions and a recent wound that had puss oozing out of it.

"Please make them stop," Alec said, the tears free flowing down his cheeks. "It's time now."

"Did they do this to you?" I whispered, pointing at the wounds. He nodded. "Do you know why they do this?" I glanced over my shoulder at the door, but it was only us.

River and Zenon wore matching facial expressions that oozed anger. I didn't blame them. Seeing the pain in Alec's face was enough for me to blast Isaac's soul out of his body without the guilt.

"They want my animal, but they don't believe me. It's already gone." Recognition registered in his eyes as he thought about something.

"Are you a shifter?" I asked gently, not wanting to scare him. I slowly stepped closer.

"I was," he said, smiling kindly, his eyes sparkling at the memory.

"Can you remember which shifter?"

"A saber-tooth tiger," he said, nodding. "We were majestic creatures back in the day." His smile reached his eyes and his cheeks blossomed red. "My brother and I used to hunt in Greenland, Antarctica, and the lands beneath. You should see the old lands one day." Alec smiled, then fell silent.

"Why did your brother leave you here?" I asked.

"It took my saber away, and then Alex grabbed the mask and he, too, changed. But his mind stayed the same. I saw too much from that mask. Too much hurt. Too much pain. Too many souls changed." He shook his head continuously, then finally settled down.

After a moment of staring at Alec, he blinked as if realizing he was speaking with us and continued, "The world within is so much better than this one. It's filled with enormous creatures and tiny insects, but all is beautiful. All is wonderful. And everybody lives peacefully. There's so much happiness there. No hurt. No pain. But we had to leave. There were explorers trying to find our home, so my brother and I thought of leaving before they hurt us, too."

He fell quiet for a moment, then added, "But we are so few now," Alec said as more tears welled in his eyes and blood drained from his face once more. His eyes glazed over as if the medication they forced down his throat had taken hold of him, and he started rocking again.

I glanced out of the window and saw three outside rooms; the fence surrounding the building and garden, and beyond that, a forest. The view was stunning. But the building that stood on this land gave me the creeps.

"What the hell is he going on about?" Zenon said, standing closer to us.

I shushed him and waved him away. "Why don't you just leave?" I said, touching Alec so he knew I was asking him a question.

He shook his head. "It wasn't the right time." He glanced nervously at the open door and whispered. His eyes finding mine. "I can't leave, and nobody can take me to the right time." He rocked. "It hasn't been time here for a while. Until now…"

A lump formed in the back of my throat, and I flinched when Alec grabbed my forearms, his fingernails digging into my skin.

"It's time," he said through dirty gritted teeth. "We must go now. Bad shifters. Bad, bad, bad."

I glanced up at Zenon and River. "Do you think we can get him out of here?"

"And take him where?" River asked, staring nervously down the hallway. "I don't like this."

"Me neither," I grumbled, and carefully removed Alec's fingernails from my forearms with Zenon's help.

"Let's try teleporting," Zenon said, grabbing Alec's shoulder and reached for my hand. When River grabbed hold of my hand and Zenon, we closed our eyes, but nothing happened.

"What's going on?" I asked, confused. "Why aren't we going anywhere?"

Zenon dropped his arms and stared at Alec from head to toe. He glanced around the room; at the old bed frame and faded blue duvet set. "Do you remember when we entered the institute it only mentions Isaac from 1946. Why aren't there others who managed the institute until our present day in 2023?"

I remembered thinking the same thing when we arrived. I glanced at Alec again. "Alec, do you know what year it is?"

"It's 1964," he said, his eyes boring a hole inside my head. "Alex thought it was a safe time. But it's not. Bad time."

An icy feeling washed over me that my suspicion was correct. "How did we get to this time, and how did you get here?" I pointed at Zenon, "When did our world change to the past?"

"It must be the tomb," Zenon said. "And then when we came to the institute based on the picture in the locket, something shifted." He shrugged.

"You mean time shifted?" I asked, frowning. "As in time traveling?"

"The real question we should ask is, how do we get back?" River asked, rubbing his face.

"If I knew that, we wouldn't be arguing about it," Zenon growled. His irritation with River was clear.

I stepped between the two and pushed them farther apart. "Let's first get out of here safely before you two fight each other. I don't know about you, but I don't want these people probing me." I glanced at Alec, who now stared out of the window and continued rocking in his chair.

"Agreed," River said, then stared at Zenon. "Let's get out of here, then you can go back to hating me."

Zenon grunted his approval and opened the window. "Let's climb—"

The mere mention of climbing set Alec off, and he began shaking and sweating. At least we knew he still listened, even though it didn't look like it. His eyes rolled into the back of his head, and he started convulsing violently. His head smacked against the chairback, and his hands hit the armrest. River grabbed him before he crashed to the floor.

"What's wrong with him?" River asked as he carefully placed Alec on his bed.

"I don't know, but he obviously doesn't enjoy climbing."

"Let's carry him down," Zenon said, crossing the room toward the door. "I don't enjoy sitting here. What if they come after us?"

"I don't like this either," I said, standing beside him. "And if they see us carrying him down, they might attack." I glanced over my shoulder and Alec was in the fetal position on his bed, sucking his thumb. "And I don't think he's in any position to go anywhere."

I opened my mouth to say we should take our chances and carry him down the stairs, bolt out of the front door and steal a car when Isaac came around the corner with an orderly and two large male nurses. They marched in unison toward us with purpose; their expressions were scary.

"It's time for Alec to receive his daily treatment," Isaac yelled down the hallway, getting closer.

Alec whimpered and wet the bed.

"I think it's time you left," Isaac grumbled, pushing River out of the way. "If you weren't able to get any information out of him by now, I highly doubt you will. He needs to go downstairs for his treatment." Isaac pointed to where the nurses and orderly were to grab him. They picked him up and carried him down the corridor and disappeared down the stairs.

Isaac turned on his heel and followed them, his welcoming demeanor long gone and in its place was contempt.

We gawked at the way they handled poor Alec and shoulder bumped Zenon, jerking my chin in their direction.

"We have to help him," I whispered. Those reptiles had better hearing than Zenon and I didn't want them hearing me.

"No, we don't," he said through gritted teeth. "What we're doing is putting our lives in danger."

"You mean a big scary vampire-were-leopard is afraid of danger."

Zenon growled, revealing his sharp teeth.

I poked him in the side, and he flinched.

"Stop being a baby and let's do something. You're apparently the big brother," when I said big brother I used air quotes, "so act like it. We're good people and don't you forget it or I'm telling Mommy."

"I hate it when you do that," he said, his tone deep and throaty. All the hairs on my arms and at the back of my neck stood up, making me shiver.

"See, all we needed was to bring those monsters of yours out to come play." I grinned and turned to River. "Are you going to join me or complain like a princess over there?"

River laughed and said, "Well, you won't catch me backing out of a fight." His flames flashed before our eyes, bathing us in heat, and then it quickly receded.

Zenon snapped his teeth and growled.

"Okay, okay, enough," I slapped Zenon on his rock-hard abdomen. He didn't flinch, but he stood straighter, "see, that wasn't so hard. Now let's go get him."

By the time we reached the bottom of the stairs, the hallway was deadly quiet. The nurse who first greeted us was no longer at the front desk, and the other rooms downstairs seemed locked or empty.

The only place left that we thought they could've gone to were the outside rooms we noticed from the upstairs window. We traversed down the porch stairs, crossed the large, neatly cut lawn out back, and approached the rooms carefully.

There were about three or four rooms next to each other, reminding me of old stables they had converted into rooms. The wooden doors were closed, but we tried the first one when we were sure there was nobody inside. The last thing we wanted to do was to surprise the reptiles while they were busy; they were a grumpy, hungry bunch.

Zenon opened it with a shove of his shoulder against the wood, almost breaking it. We entered the ammonia smelling room; one side of the room had shelves filled with various surgical instruments that would give me nightmares. Against the far wall was a shiny silver surgical table with clean clamps, forceps, scalpels, a speculum, and even a bone cutter on a tray.

"What are they doing to these children?" I asked, speaking more to myself than the men.

"Whatever it is, it's not pretty," River said beside me. His tone filled with a quiet rage. "No idea what they'd use this for?" He touched a large cylinder-type-gas-bottle with glass in front to show the level; the bottle was empty.

Screams sounded in the room next door, and we froze in our respective spots. Then Zenon moved so fast I barely saw him until his spot was empty and was already outside, peering through tiny slits above their door.

We joined him outside and listened to the screaming. Alec cried out, begging them to stop. A whistle sounded and something clanked against the floors, then they scraped an object across the cement ground, bringing it closer. The screaming continued, forcing me to block my ears.

Alec's high-pitched screams added to my anxiety, and I shook my head in quiet anger. I couldn't handle the pain he was experiencing along with his screams, and I wanted to blast through the door and kill the men hurting him. He screamed again, and I choked on a sob. They were hurting him and his cries for help struck my core.

'*We have to help,*' I mouthed. While River stared at me with angry flames in his eyes. We could take them. We could kill Isaac and his men. I knew deep in my heart we could rescue Alec from these terrible lizard shifters.

Zenon stepped away from the slits above the door, his face now pale. He was a tanned were-leopard and he never paled. Even his yellow/golden eyes had darkened.

I shrugged and mouthed, '*What is it?*'

Zenon shook his head.

The screams abruptly ended. A cylinder clanked against the floor and rolled. They spoke as metal struck metal and there was movement.

We were too late... even if we had broken down the door, Alec may not have lived for much longer and we would've risked our lives. Although I didn't know Alec, I'd just met the man, but I felt bad for what he'd gone through.

River shoved me out of the way and into Zenon, and we entered the next vacant room; the door had stood wide open. As I closed the wooden door, it creaked, forcing me to let go of the door not to alert them of our presence.

Isaac exited the room the moment I let go of the creaking door; he walked upright in his crocodile-like-lizard-body, holding up two large vials of blood. "Don't forget to send the cleaners there," he said nonchalantly, thumbing behind him.

"Yes, boss," said the two nurses and orderly at the same time. They walked beside him as their natural lizard selves. Their tails swished left and right as they laughed and joked about what they had done to Alec. Their large bodies stomped across the backyard, and they disappeared inside the institute.

"What the actual f—"

"No swearing," River said, interrupting my bout of swear words. "Let's see what they did."

"No," I said, "we don't want to see his demise."

"Suit yourself."

Not wanting to be left behind, I joined the two men and entered the next room with them but could go no farther than the doorjamb. The coppery smell of Alec's blood assaulted my senses as my eyes bounced around the room; blood splattered against the walls and ceiling, with blood dripping onto the floor. I dared not look at the bed Alec was on. And in the far-right corner stood three full cylinders.

"What do you think they were doing with his blood and the cylinders?" I asked, wanting to go near them and open one to see, but my feet couldn't move.

"Are you sure you want to find out?" Zenon said, brushing against my shoulder as he entered the room. "You know you'll only have nightmares."

"I know," I said sadly, recalling the time when after I returned home following my stint working with Victor and River. The things I'd witnessed that night would leave me scarred for life; the brutality and waste of it all. I shut my eyes tight as the memory surfaced.

"I need to know what they were doing to him," my eyes finally darted to Alec's torn, bloody body, and I swallowed hard, "why they had to hurt him so badly is beyond me. But he's at peace now." I choked on the last words and wiped my eyes.

Zenon and River approached the full cylinders, and they each grabbed one, turning the valves at the same time. Screams pierced our ears, and they quickly closed them. We stood staring at each other like our world had just shattered. I didn't want us hanging around here any longer. The lizards might return, and they would do the same to us.

"What are they doing capturing someone's scream?" I asked nervously, glancing back at the large institute, but didn't see any movement near any of the windows.

"Maybe they feed off of them," River said, his face paler than usual. "Maybe they enjoy the demise of others."

"We have to get out of here," I said. "I really don't want to be tortured and sound like that." I pointed at the cylinders and stepped farther back.

"Agreed, but can we teleport, or must we walk home?" Zenon said, approaching the bed Alec's body was on. He inspected the wounds inflicted on his abdomen, chest and neck, careful not to touch his blood. He sniffed near the corpse. "His blood smells different," Zenon said, wrinkling his nose. "It's sweeter in some areas and fowl smelling in others. Strange."

"That's fascinating, but please can we get out of here before they return," I said, peering out of the door again, but nobody was coming to us.

"Let's go," River said, grabbing my shoulder and touching Zenon's arm.

Chapter Twelve

The world darkened around me and when I opened my eyes; we were inside the tomb once more. My stomach recoiled, and my breakfast from this morning threatened to repeat on me. I fell to my knees from the sudden shift and teleportation, breathing in deeply.

Zenon leaned against the wall, trying to catch his breath, while River doubled over and coughed, spitting out blood. His skull was aflame, but there were more dull blue flames than his usual bright yellow and red ones.

"What's with this place?" I asked, climbing to my feet on shaky legs. "I thought we were going home, not back here," I grumbled.

"I thought of your home too," River said, his body still burning.

"And you've brought me along for the sick ride. Now I'm stuck too," Zenon moaned, dusting his clothing.

Whatever was going on, we had to see it positively; there had to be a reason we kept coming back to the tomb. "At least I bring excitement to your life." I tried for humor, but

Zenon wasn't budging. "If you were back home, you'd be playing online games with your buddies."

"I have a job," Zenon said, his tone harsh.

River coughed, and his flames slowly receded. He stretched out his back and Luna barked, running up to him. River bent on one knee and rubbed his best friend, and she licked his hands, fingers, and face.

"What now?" Zenon said wearily, pulling me out of my thoughts.

I blinked and turned toward him. "Honestly, I don't know. We went to see Alec but got no answers. All that happened is we heard a man being tortured by lizard shifters."

"What about the locket?" he asked, holding out his hand.

I pulled it out of my bag and remembered the book I'd taken from the professor's office and pulled that out, too. I placed both items on the sarcophagus. "Didn't we leave this open?" I asked.

"Yeah, but we seemed to go through time wormholes or something. Nothing is as it seems," Zenon said, approaching. "And this is probably another time in another dimension." He shooed me away. "Let's see what you got here," he opened the book, "just great... a journal." He opened the locket and frowned. "The picture has changed, though. There's a little boy, Harry, with Alec at the institute. It looks like some sort of magic show." Zenon showed me the locket and pointed at the boy's name sewn into his clothing.

The locket revealed clues to our next destination, and I groaned; I didn't want to go back to the institute. "There has to be another way," I said, closing the locket. "If we go back to the institute, we'll just get caught by the lizards. And besides, it's probably just showing us a memory of Alec with this boy Harry."

"We'll probably go to that time and the lizards won't know about us because it's in the past," River said, frowning.

"Wait," Zenon said, holding up his hands. "I agree, we can't go back to the Institute. We've learned all we need to know about what goes on there and the lizards probably hurt that child, too. And if he's still alive, he is not well for surviving that place. There has to be something here." He turned on his heels and carefully looked at the walls within the tomb. He took his time dusting the sand off the hieroglyphics and mumbled to himself.

Zenon had not only aged quickly soon after his birth, but he had also absorbed information like one breathed air. He had read every book he could get his hands on and remembered each word in a sentence on every page. He was one of those brilliant minds, except this one came with an attitude.

He walked around the tomb once more and then pushed the heavy lid off the sarcophagus. "He looks different," he said, pointing at the mummy.

I approached to see what he was talking about. River stayed in the corner with Luna. His face had become more gaunt than before. I wanted to say something but didn't think he would tell me the truth; that he was dying with my father. I blinked back unshed tears and swallowed hard. Then I smiled when Luna placed her goofy head on River's leg, her long tongue hanging out of one side of her mouth.

Movement beside me caught my attention. I closed the gap and peered over the side of the sarcophagus to see what Zenon was looking at. The mummy was undisturbed. Nobody had ever moved his body since they put him there.

There was sand all around him and parts of the linen had fallen away from his face, revealing his mummified features. But where there was nothing before, now under his left arm was the remains of a case.

"No idea what to make of this," I said with a sigh.

Zenon rubbed his face. "Do we have all the information? Shouldn't we ask Victor exactly what had happened? River might have heard wrong and we're trying to solve a puzzle by playing broken telephone."

"Your father isn't doing well," River whispered, ignoring Zenon's jab. He coughed again and pressed his head against the wall.

"What's going on?" I asked and approached. "Tell me the truth." I crouched beside him and rubbed Luna's head.

"Victor is dying, and so will I if we don't solve this." River looked at me with those warm amber-brown-colored eyes. He scratched the stubble on his chin and sighed, wincing every time he moved. "I don't think I can go anywhere," he nodded in Zenon's direction, "but your brother can help you. The two of you can do this."

River burst into his angry flames as if trying to conserve his human energy. Luna burned with her owner as they sat there resting.

"How much time do we have?" I asked.

River shrugged. "Can't anymore," he whispered. His dark orb eyes flickered gray and his once bright red and yellow flames became dull.

River and I had our problems, but I still loved him, and it pained me to witness his demise.

The back of my throat ached and as much as I didn't want to say it, I would miss him if anything happened to him. "Don't worry, we'll find the mask," I said with determination in my voice. I needed River to know that we could do this and before time ran out.

"There has to be something else in this tomb that can help us." I stood, giving River and Luna space.

River pulled something out of his pocket; the newspaper clipping. I took it out of his flaming phalanges.

"That's the professor and here's his brother," I pointed at the two men who were closest to the camera, "but who is this?" I pointed at the man in the background holding a box. I'd been so focused on the professor and the sarcophagus that I didn't notice the other men. The fact that Alec had been in the photo all along left me angry with myself for not seeing it before. But then again, neither River nor Zenon noticed it, too. We needed to find the other two men. Perhaps they could help us.

"That looks like the box that's now in the sarcophagus," Zenon said, taking the clipping out of my hand.

"It looks similar." I peered inside the sarcophagus again, looking at the box there and the one in the clipping. "Yep, same box."

"Let's find this guy," Zenon said, pointing at the man in the back. "He has to know something."

"But how? We don't even know what time we're in or who he is." I moaned as I reached for Zenon's hand.

"Focus on him," he pointed at the man again, "and then when we teleport, that's all we think about. We must land somewhere near him."

River coughed again and his burning skeleton flared to life, then settled down to a gentle burn, but his skeleton started turning gray. We had nothing to lose. We had to try.

"Fine, brother, let's do this."

Chapter Thirteen

We landed softly in an alley right beside a dumpster. The smell of urine and rotten food assaulted my olfactory senses, and I blocked my nose.

"Where are we?" I asked, following Zenon toward the sidewalk. "It looks like Sterling Meadow." We approached the same movie theaters I used to frequent as a teenager, the coffee shop Mom and I enjoyed many breakfasts, although the signage on the glass was brighter than I was used to.

I paid for a newspaper and my finger hovered over the date, my finger shaking. "No... why are we here and now?" I asked nobody but Zenon looked over my shoulder and harrumphed.

"I should've known that stupid tomb would send us here," he grumbled.

We had arrived in Sterling Meadow in 1988. I hadn't even been born yet. I threw the newspaper into the trashcan with force; it smacked into a glass bottle, making an awful sound.

I exhaled slowly with my hands on my hips and turned

around in a circle, getting a good look at our surroundings. Coffee shop. Movie theatre. Shops. Theater. More shops. I turned back and glanced up at the big yellow sign that read 'See Harry 'Houdini' Morris Magic Show.'

I slapped Zenon's stomach, and he barely flinched. He glanced up at the sign I was staring at and whistled. "Maybe we need to go inside?" Zenon said, heading for the ticket counter without waiting for my reply.

I stomped inside the main entrance of the theater. Zenon paid for our tickets and handed me mine. We approached the ticket agent, who checked our tickets and pointed toward our seats.

"I'm hating that secret tomb more and more," I grumbled as we entered.

"Don't get your panties in a bunch. I'm with you and together we'll solve this. Imagine we see Mom." He chuckled. "I'd love to see her hairstyle in the eighties, but don't tell her we were here."

I glanced up at him with smiling eyes. "She'll have a hernia if she found out we were time hopping or dimension hopping or whatever that tomb does to us." I rubbed my tired face. "But don't you think it's amazing how the tomb knows where we need to go without us knowing."

Zenon stopped walking and stared at me like I'd sprouted a flower out of my ear. "We need to find someone who can give us more information on that tomb."

"Well, we're in town and Léon is Master Vampire. He knows all things Egyptian, and if not, he will find out. Maybe we can chat with him when the show is over." I was silent for a second, then added, "How come you know nothing about it, though. You're supposed to be Mister-Know-It-All?" I rolled my eyes.

He bumped into my shoulder playfully. "I don't know

everything, miss smarty pants. Anyway, Léon will know what to do." He thought for a moment. "Do you know I've entered none of his warehouses? Maybe I should see what artifacts he has stored when we get back to our time."

"No," I said, raising my hand. "I don't want you unleashing a thousand-year-old virus into the air or worse, discovering an ancient vampire clan that nobody can kill." I shuddered at the thought. "We've had enough bad news for one century."

Zenon just stared at me. "Stop watching so much Sci-Fi, it's melting your brain." He poked my head with his long index finger.

"Rubbish," I said, swatting his hand away. "I get out."

"No, you don't. You need friends."

"I have friends," I said, frowning.

"Reading books is not considered friends."

"That's what you think; reading is not only good for your soul but transports you to different worlds. You learn new languages and about new people. It's magical. You should try it sometime. You just might learn something new."

"Shush, the show is about to start."

I rolled my eyes. He knew I was right, and I knew for a fact that he enjoyed reading as much as I did, but he would never say that. My baby brother was much too proud to admit he loved reading as much as he enjoyed f—.

Zenon yanked on my arm, bringing me out of my thoughts. I smiled knowingly and wondered if he could read minds, too. Although Léon wasn't his biological father, he could read minds and thought it would be great if Zenon had some of the vampire's traits too.

We entered the theater and found our seats right at the back. The smell of popcorn wafted in the air with a low hum of whispering as excitement grew to watch the magic show. They had filled almost every seat and on stage stood the magician and his assistant waiting patiently for the audience to quieten down.

Once the theater was quiet, Harry 'Houdini' Morris welcomed everybody. He started the show with the disappearing object trick and then proceeded to do a card trick.

I elbowed Zenon and jerked my chin in the magician's direction; he looked exactly like the man in the newspaper clipping. And he looked like every magician I'd ever seen; short, neat hair, cleanly shaven, and wearing a tuxedo.

Zenon glanced at the newspaper clipping and at the magician and nodded. It was definitely him, and I was grateful we didn't waste time wandering around the streets of Sterling Meadow looking for clues. We had found him here.

Harry had long fingers I struggled to monitor, and as much as I despised magicians, his show was entertaining. Zenon yawned beside me like he'd seen every trick in the book. While I was struggling with the idea that he had doves in his hat. This was my first actual show; I'd seen snippets of magicians on television, but I'd never watched one in a theatre before. Zenon, on the other hand, had seen everything and had been everywhere already. He was hungry for information.

If we were alone, I might have smacked him; for someone who had travelled the world, he seemed as stumped as I was at this mystery we found ourselves in.

The show captivated the audience; me included. Both Harry and his assistant, Myles, wore matching black coats, the inside was a bright red, that billowed behind them as they walked with purpose for each trick. In my humble opinion, they orchestrated each trick carefully and magically.

"Do you think they use real magic?" I whispered near Zenon's ear.

Zenon was quiet as he watched, but I knew he heard me. "The theatre is humming with a quiet type of magic, but yes," he said, nodding, "I think they are using magic."

I nodded, even though he couldn't see me. I felt the slight buzz of something. Unsure what it was exactly, but I felt something that was akin to magic and could explain why their show was so good.

When it was over an hour later, we waited for everybody to leave before approaching the stage. Harry and Myles had already started packing their belongings.

"Do you only have the one show in Sterling Meadow?" I asked when I got near the stage.

Harry and Myles spun around, unaware that anybody had stayed behind. "Uh, hi, yes," Harry stammered and closed the distance. Myles turned his back to us and continued packing.

"Your show was great," I said, proffering my hand to shake his. "I'm Scout, and this is my brother, Zenon."

Harry shook our hands with a smile plastered on his face; it was the same smile he gave his audience. His eyes flittered from Zenon to me.

"What can I do for you?" Harry said, squatting, and continued smiling.

"Can you tell us anything about this newspaper clipping?" I retrieved the picture out of my bag and showed it to him.

Harry stared at it for a long time, then squinted. He stood, elbowing Myles and showing him the clipping. "This date is set in the future," Harry said with a puzzled look. "I look older," he added. His brows pushing together in confusion.

"Yes, in 2023," I started, then gave him a short version of what we'd been through. As I spoke, they invited us to join them in their change rooms while they continued packing their things and listening. Zenon and I sat on one sofa sipping the hot tea Myles had made while Zenon finished the cookies.

Once I finished the story, both men sat across from us.

"I honestly don't know what to say," Harry finally said. "This is the future you're talking about. I don't know what's going to happen between now and 2023." He glanced at Myles, who shrugged in response.

"Can you confirm it is you in the background?" I asked Myles, pointing at a blurry face in the newspaper clipping. In the far corner, a person who looked like Myles stood with his arms folded. I couldn't see his face clearly, but from what I'd seen here now, how he walked around and behaved, his demeanor in the photo seemed off. Maybe…

"Can't tell, but," Myles said, looking more closely, "it could be."

"I'm not aware of any Mask of Immortality, although it does sound intriguing." Harry glanced at Myles with a smile I could only describe as sly. "Maybe we should start looking for it."

Something registered in Myles's expression, and I wondered whether we didn't plant the idea in their heads. But it didn't matter if they heard it from us now or if they would hear about it in the future, anyway. Either way, both men were involved with its discovery. Regardless of when, the men couldn't help us now. They wouldn't know what had happened at the tomb or what happened to the mask, and they knew nothing about the professor, his death, or his brother.

Zenon glanced at me, his eyes flicking to the side, letting me know he wanted to leave. We stood up.

"I don't think you can help us now," I said, pocketing the newspaper clipping and pulling my satchel over my head. "We're leaving. Thank you for your time, and perhaps we see you again in the future," I said, smiling, but it didn't reach my eyes.

"Yes, perhaps," Harry said, proffering a hand.

Myles tipped his head in greeting and continued packing.

Zenon and I thanked them for their time and headed for the exit.

"What I can't understand is why the magician is young now, yet old, in the photo, but Myles looks the same," I said, shielding my eyes from the sun when we walked outside.

"No idea. But either we put the idea in their head or they are good liars," Zenon said, pointing left and we headed that way, traversing the sidewalk and passing a bookstore.

"I was thinking the same thing. Now what?" I asked with my hands on my hips. "I don't know what to do now," I sighed, exhaustion taking hold of me.

"I want to follow them," Zenon said, crossing the street.

Chapter Fourteen

Zenon ordered lunch while I freshened up in the bathroom. When I returned and sat down, the magician and his assistant stood on the sidewalk waiting for someone.

"Sorry," Zenon called our server over, "can we get these to go?"

"Yes, sir," she said, leaving us alone.

"But I'm hungry," I moaned, taking a bite of my sandwich. "I hate eating on the go."

"Quit moaning. We don't do this often."

The server returned, handing Zenon two empty boxes and the bill. He packed our lunch into the boxes, and left money on the table, making the server blush at the tip.

"I forget we're in 1988," Zenon said, walking quickly and eating. "Anyway, at least the server will have a good day." He pointed at the closest cab, and we climbed inside. "Follow that car," he said, making the cab driver smile.

"Yes, sir," the cab driver said. "I've always wanted to do this." He put the car into gear and smashed the gas.

"Not too close," Zenon said in between mouthfuls. "We

don't want to spook them. Maintain one car between us and them."

"Yes, sir," he said. I glanced at the name tag stuck on the dashboard and it read Nelson.

I sat in the backseat eating my lunch while the cab driver swerved, applying speed, then slowing down. I was worried I'd get car sick if he continued like this.

We followed the magician and his assistant for about twenty minutes and parked a block away from where they had stopped. The men climbed out of their ride, grabbed their belongings, and entered an apartment building.

"Isn't that one of Léon's building?" I asked, frowning. Léon owned various apartment buildings all over Sterling Meadow and his vampires mainly used them. If the magician and his assistant lived here, then one of them had to be a vampire or they knew someone who was. Which made little sense because both walked in daylight, and they didn't burst into a cloud of flames and dust.

"Yeah," Zenon said, paying Nelson.

"Thank you, sir. Do you want me to stay here and wait in case you need to go somewhere else?"

"No," — Zenon said, slapping Nelson on the shoulder, — "but thanks anyway. We'll find our way back."

"Sure thing," he said.

We climbed out and approached the ominous building. Dark clouds had gathered, bathing the property in shadows. The gargoyles on each of the top corners screamed silently and followed us with their hollow eyes as we neared. I shook off the icy feeling of being watched and chalked it up to nerves of steel I didn't have. Not yet anyway. And with Dad being gravely ill, I doubted I would level up in the power department any time soon since he was the gatekeeper.

Although I'd been working with Mom and Ralph at

their Ulysses Assassins business for a year, I still had a lot to learn about all the monsters that roamed the earth. Therefore, some sinister creatures still frightened me; like those gargoyles glaring down at us.

We entered the vampire-only building, and it relieved me it was still daylight, which meant no vampire would be out of their apartment and licking their lips. I'd never had a vampire munch on me before, but there was always a first time for everything. But I had nothing to worry about because the vampires should be dead to the world until nightfall; fingers crossed.

The entrance doors swung shut with a soft clank and the dim lights in the foyer were enough for us to see our way, but not bright enough to read the signs on the walls. I squinted, making out the words *'Enter at Own Risk'*.

"Just great," I mumbled softly to myself.

I flinched when I heard footsteps above us.

"Stairs," Zenon whispered, pointing in the direction we had to go.

"I wonder who they're here to see," I whispered, taking two steps at a time as quietly as possible.

"I would've preferred to see Léon first, but that can wait." He stopped on the second floor and blocked me from going up the next flight. "They're down there," he said, pointing to the left.

"You're better than a bloodhound," I said, grinning.

"Of course. I'm even better than my father." His grin matching mine.

"Does Sebastian know you lie?" I whispered, stepping faster out of his grasp or he'd pinch my shoulder like he always did. I turned the corner and almost walked into the back of Myles when Zenon grabbed me with his super-fast moves and pulled me against him.

My heart threatened to burst out of my chest from almost getting caught by them. We stayed frozen to the spot around the corner as we listened. Nothing. They didn't hear us behind them, and Zenon slowly let go of my jaw. I groaned inwardly because he covered my mouth with his dirty hands, and I tasted old mayonnaise. I held my breath and gave a tiny shudder, wiping my mouth clean.

I turned around slowly and pointed at Zenon's hands and mouthed, *'dirty'*, and wiped my mouth for effect. Zenon laughed at my expense and pressed his index finger to my mouth to shush me. Me being the oldest between the two, I stuck my tongue out at him. He rolled his eyes. Zenon gently pushed me to his other side as we listened to the men talk to someone in a nearby apartment.

"…just tell him that someone is on to us and the sooner we find out who is spilling the beans, the better. And it's not just us time-hopping," Myles said angrily, making my arms pebble.

I glanced up at Zenon, who pressed his index finger to his lips, shushing me again. I frowned. I wasn't naïve, and this wasn't my first case. When Harry spoke, I stilled and listened intently.

"We want more money for our trouble."

"He has graced you with your youth, and you're able to stay in this time with no repercussions," a man said and I didn't recognize his voice. I assumed he was the vampire who lived in the apartment. If he was awake now, long before sunset, that meant he was powerful. "So, I would shut up about money if I were you, and if you get caught, it's your problem. I think my employer has already paid you handsomely. So," the man said as the door creaked, "not my problem."

"But—" Harry complained when someone started choking and spitting.

"One thing I hate," said the voice. "Is repeating myself. Now, do I make myself clear, or should I smite the two of you here and now?"

"No, no," Myles stammered. "We get it. Don't worry. We just wanted to warn you, that's all. Isn't that right, Harry?"

"Good," said the voice.

Harry coughed.

Someone patted a back.

"Now," the voice continued. "The professor and his brother are dead. So there are no other loose ends unless you two give me trouble. The reptilians are on our side, and if we need an army, they can help us now or in the future, if needed. One thing I want you to understand is nobody, and I mean nobody, informs my employer of any issues. And certainly not about Victor's daughter. Do not mutter her name to anybody. I'm here to sort it out for my employer. Now don't fuck this up, Harry."

A slap sounded, followed by someone wincing.

"Yes, we understand," Harry said, sounding wounded. "Is there anything we can do about the girl?"

"Leave. Her. Alone. And do nothing except leave town today and continue with your stupid shows like you begged for. If I ever need you again, I'll find you." The door abruptly slammed closed.

Zenon pointed at an open door across the hallway and we entered the tiny kitchen. They mainly used the small kitchen for their vending machine full of blood bags. I shuddered at the thought and was grateful I didn't need to drink any blood to survive. Zenon, on the other hand, looked starving. He rarely drank blood, unless offered and fresh out of the willing female.

Footsteps neared, and the men descended the stairs in icy silence.

"Do you think we should knock on his door?" I asked, peering around the corner at the apartment. "He will lead us to the person responsible for all this."

"No," Zenon said, shaking his head. "That vampire is powerful, and I don't think we can take him by ourselves. We need to speak with Léon first. He can definitely help us with him."

"Okay," I said, turning back to find Zenon staring at the vending machine and licking his lips. I pushed him out of the tiny kitchen and pointed toward the apartment. "I want to see which number it is." We approached the offending apartment only to find it didn't have a number on the door, but there were remnants of part of the number that was left behind.

I went to the apartment next door, and it was 87, the next was 89, and the one after that was 91. Odd numbers. I joined Zenon again, who kept glancing at the tiny kitchen.

"No, that's bad old blood and most likely synthetic. Let's go to Léon. I'm sure he can give you fresh blood out of his human tap."

"Ugh, you're so gross," he said. "What number was his?"

"It's 85."

We traversed down the stairs, ensuring no vampire or magician and assistant was about to corner us and exited the apartment building.

Chapter Fifteen

The one place we were certain we'd find Léon, Master Vampire of Sterling Meadow, would be at the Labyrinth; his impenetrable wall shifting building guarded by werewolves, were-rats, were-leopards, and sometimes were-tigers. The vampires within the walls they protected belonged to Léon's kiss.

The cab stopped outside the heavily guarded entrance, and we climbed out. I paid for the ride this time.

"You do realize they will think we're off our rocker," I said, stopping Zenon from going farther.

"What do you mean? That we're from the future?"

"Exactly. No were-animal or vampire is going to believe us."

"They'll realize when we tell them." Zenon approached the building, and I yanked on his arm to stop. "Ow, what is it?" he yelled.

"What if we're messing with the future by speaking to them in the past?" I asked with concern in my voice.

Zenon stared at me like I was crazy, then glanced over

his shoulder at his home in the future. His shoulders sagged. "But that's just it… we don't know. This could be a different time dimension, and the Léon we speak with now isn't our Léon from the future. And whatever we say now won't affect anything in our past or future."

Now it was my turn to stare at him like he was nuts. "What?" I rubbed my temples. "You're making my head hurt."

"Well, that took little," he said, smiling.

I lowered my hands to my sides and glowered up at him.

"Easy there, tiger," he said, reaching for my shoulders and squeezed. "To minimize any damage, let's ask to just see Léon out here. That way, we don't have to interact with anyone, really. And you know Léon as much as I do. He's discreet and knowing, and if this gives him an edge for the future, then so be it. But we have to try. We are literally out of ideas."

He was right, and my thoughts went back to River and Victor, who were dying. I nodded once, agreeing with his sentiment.

"Good, now let's go," Zenon said, spinning around and knocked the secret knock.

Elena, the scary were-rat, yanked the door open and greeted us with an angry frown. "What do you want?" she asked.

Elena was one of those nice were-rats who, when pushed too far, could tear your head from your body in a matter of seconds, but at the same time, was a surrogate mother to anyone who had become lost in this cruel world or were slightly broken. When she first opened the door, her expression went from *'who the hell are you'* to *'oh my gods… you two are familiar'*. Then her frown returned.

Elena considered us for a moment, then spoke. "Who are you here to see?"

"Could you call Léon, please—"

"Do you have an appointment?" Elena asked, interrupting me.

"We don't have an appointment," Zenon added in his smooth, melt a woman's panties tone. "But it's pertinent that we speak with him immediately," Zenon said with a smoldering look, reminding me of Flynn Rider.

Elena stared at him with bored eyes, then glanced at me. "Does that usually work?"

"I assume so," I said, trying not to smile.

"I see…" she glanced from Zenon to me. "You two siblings?"

"Yes," I said, nodding and still trying not to smile.

"Your brother is charming, but he's wasting his time on me. Anyway," her eyes flitted from mine to Zenon, "let me see what I can do, but I can't promise anything."

"Thank you," I said kindly. "I know it's still light, but he should wake for the day soon and if he wouldn't mind seeing us out here."

Elena's eyebrows shot up in surprise. "Stay here," she grumbled, closing the door behind her with a loud slam and hurried away.

"Well… that went smoothly."

"Hahahaha," I laughed. "You are so smooth, baby brother."

"Shut up."

We waited about half an hour when the door opened abruptly. Léon stood in the doorjamb with his arms crossed over his broad chest. His dark features seemed sinister in the gloomy blackness of the Labyrinth.

"Who are you, and what do you want?"

Chapter Sixteen

Zenon and I spoke at the same time. Léon raised both hands to shush us. "Before I drain you both of blood, one at a time, please, you're hurting my ears." I'd never seen Léon so grumpy before, then I remembered he didn't know who we were and doubted he cared. I had to remind myself that Léon was a vampire who had just woken up and, most likely hungry.

I told Zenon to go first, and he informed Léon as quickly as possible about what had happened until now. The Master Vampire considered his words, but I knew he thought we were mad; I would if I was in his shoes.

"We know one of your powers is reading minds. So... read our minds," I said quickly, "as proof of what he said."

"I believe you, little one," Léon said, raising his hand to shush me. "I might not remember you now, but I'm sure in my future I will remember this day as it unfolds right now in our present." He exhaled even though he didn't need to and rubbed his temples.

"This is most strange," he finally said. His dark blue

colored eyes staring suspiciously at us, as he remained in the shadows of his home. "But… I have heard of this Mask of Immortality and forbid anyone to seek it out. If Victor is in danger, that means you're in danger," he pointed at me, "and you need help. But you," he pointed at Zenon, "who are you and how do you fit into this puzzle?"

Zenon hesitated and glanced at me.

"Just tell him," I said with a shrug. "If he reads our minds, I'm sure he'll find out, anyway."

Léon frowned; it was the first time I'd seen the vampire's expression change from that carved from stone demeanor to one of confusion.

"In the future, you're one of my father's," Zenon blurted that out so fast I barely heard a word. "And she's my sister." He pointed at me.

I added that he and Sebastian, his brother, were still currently dating our mother.

Léon's expression changed back to that one that made him look dead to the world, and then he swallowed hard; I watched his Adam's apple bob up and down.

"I see," Léon said, rubbing his lips like he had a mustache, but there wasn't even stubble. He was clearly dumbstruck by the news. "The future hasn't happened yet. You are siblings with different fathers and you're hunting for the Mask of Immortality. Okay, let's continue this discussion inside," he said, turning around and disappearing down the dark hallway.

Zenon caught the door before it closed shut and we followed the vampire to his office, locking the door behind us once we entered. "I would hate for anyone to eavesdrop on our conversation."

"Too late," I mumbled, standing to one side. We had just said most of the important information outside.

Although there weren't many people in the area, any vampire or shifter could've heard us. I didn't know what else we could say that was more important in his office.

Once inside the office, I sat on a two-seater couch while Zenon sat on the single chair. Léon paced in front of us with his arms behind his back. He went behind his desk and opened a drawer. He pulled out an old tome, slamming it on his desk, making me flinch, and began paging through it.

"Am I your biological father?" Léon said, staring at Zenon.

"You don't want it to be a surprise, rather?"

Léon shook his head. "Tell me." His expression left me on edge, and I didn't want to look at him anymore.

Zenon stared at Léon for a heartbeat, then finally spoke. "Just look at me and decide for yourself who you think is my biological father."

"Sebastian?" Léon said. "Must be."

"Yes, but don't let that stop you from becoming the vampire father I need. You're just as much a dad to me as he is, if not more. You teach me a lot about being a vampire, and my love for Egypt is because of you."

A red tear twinkled in Léon's eyes, but when he blinked, it disappeared. A thin smile played on his lips as he stared at Zenon, then glanced at me. "There are some similarities between you two, and your mother must be beautiful. What she sees in me and my brother, we'll never know," he grinned. "Anyway, let's see about sorting this mess out."

Léon paged through the tome, mumbling to himself.

Zenon leaned forward, concentrating, then shrugged. I didn't think he could hear even with his super hearing.

A couple of minutes went by when Léon slammed the book shut with a groan and shook his head. "There isn't much information on the mask that we don't already know.

Only that it's to be avoided at all costs." He combed his fingers through his long, dark hair, then leaned back in his chair. His hair fell loosely around his face, framing a square jaw, high cheekbones and ocean-deep-colored eyes.

"What about the tomb?" I asked, standing up and approaching his old wooden desk framed with wrought iron. The desk was ancient, reminding me of medieval times. The portraits adorned on the wall behind him were of two men and a woman in the middle.

"The tomb is a time portal," he said, tapping his long index finger on the tome. "They have cursed the tomb with knowing what the occupants need, but only if it relates to the mask. Upon entering, it knows your destination and will take you there, but only if you can teleport. If not, then it's just another tomb where others can walk in and out of."

"How can the newspaper clipping be that of the brothers, the magician, and his assistant, yet when we were there, it was undisturbed?"

"Because you were there before they were—"

"Then where was the mask?"

"Hiding in plain sight." When neither of us responded, Léon continued explaining. "Because the secret tomb is a time portal. It wanted to show you a story, and it also wants you to solve the riddle. The mask was there all along. Before the brothers, the magician and his assistant discovered it, it was on the pharaoh's face." He raised the tomb to show us an ancient sketch of the pharaoh and how they had first placed the mask on his face, and then later transferred it to a box for safekeeping.

I glanced at Zenon with my signature confused look, and he shrugged.

"How did you not see this?" I said to Zenon. "You're supposed to know these things." I teased.

"What do we do now?" Zenon said, ignoring my jab. "Do we go back to the secret tomb and remove the mask from his mummified body?"

Léon nodded. "It's the only way. Take the mask before the others discover it, destroy it, and get back home."

"But how do we do that? If any of us touch it, it will render us mortal and we, too, will perish," I said, remembering the look on my dad's face.

It reminded me of the story of how my mom met Léon and the three jewels she handled. No vampire could touch it. When she held the three jewels together, it rendered them powerless for a moment or two. Back then, my mom didn't know what power she held, therefore thought nothing about losing her powers temporarily.

"I'd be careful," Léon said gravely. "The information provided is vague and may leave you powerless forever. Whatever you do, tread carefully, and use a weapon to destroy it."

"I guess we have to get this over and done with," Zenon said, standing up to leave. "Victor is probably worsening."

'And River', I thought and joined Zenon by the door.

"Before we go, who stays in apartment 85?" I asked, almost forgetting about the other reason we had to see Léon.

"Which apartment complex?" Léon said, confused. "I have many."

I explained which building it was along with the surrounding shops I remembered, since there weren't any names on the buildings.

Léon's eyes glowed red, then he quickly schooled his features. He knew who the vampire was living there, and it didn't look like he wanted to say who it was. "I'll take care of him," Léon said with his hand on the door handle.

"We'll need to go with you," I said, stepping closer to Zenon. If my question angered Léon, then I'd need help.

Léon shook his head slowly as he considered my request. "I can't have you in the area when I question him. It will turn ugly. He is dangerous."

"He has information on who started this. If we can't accompany you, you ask him questions and allow us to wait for you before we return to the secret tomb," I said with pleading eyes and hoped it worked.

Léon pinched the bridge of his nose. "Is she always like this?" he asked Zenon, who nodded. "Your mother is probably like that too." Zenon and I grinned. "No need to answer. We go at night and you must remain where I tell you to. Understood?" He cautioned. "I don't want either of you hurt. It will just mess something up in the timeline."

"I swear," I said, smiling.

Chapter Seventeen

I shivered beside Zenon, who stood like a statue, watching the apartment building across the road.

"It's so unfair," I grumbled. "We should be there."

"No, you just want to fight."

"No, I want to ask that vampire questions before Léon destroys him."

Zenon side-eyed me.

"Fine, I also want to fight," I said, grinning up at him like a cat who ate the bird.

"You're terrible."

"Incorrigible," I corrected.

"Let's go look," Zenon said mischievously and crossed the road.

I ran after him, giddy with excitement.

"Come, child, but be quiet."

I slapped his shoulder. "I'm not a child."

"Whatever, move it and be quiet. Your shoes are loud on the tiles."

Zenon opened the door to the apartment building, and I

tiptoed in behind him. I padded quietly across the tiled floor and metaphorically patted myself on the back. "See, they're soft," I whispered and pointed at my sneakers.

Zenon rolled his eyes and headed left instead of to the right and up the stairs. He placed his index finger on his lips to shush me and pointed, mouthing the words *'other stairs'*.

I gave him a thumbs up.

As we turned the corner, a kiss of vampires stood in a circle ravaging their newly purchased blood bags. They stopped sucking on the plastic, raising their heads and sniffed. Their eyes bled over into a savage red and their fangs elongated further.

There had to be something in Zenon's scent because they didn't bat an eyelash at him; they all gazed hungrily at me.

"We're under Léon's protection, boys," Zenon said, thinking quick on his feet. "If anyone touches a hair on her head, he will destroy you." He grabbed my hand and pulled me to his right-hand side as we passed them.

"We'll see about that," said the vampire closest to us and the other two hissed; red spittle dripping down their chins.

"Ask him yourself," Zenon said, pointing upstairs, "he's over there."

"Why?" the vampire farthest from us said. "He never comes here himself."

"One of you pissed him off," I said, a little too smugly. "Who knows, maybe you're next?"

Zenon squeezed my hand a little too hard, and pulled me along behind him as we traversed up the other set of stairs to the first floor. The three vampires continued sucking on their blood bags, but I felt their dark gaze on me like I was dessert.

"Must you tease them?" Zenon said, letting go of my hand once we reached the first floor.

"What?" I shrugged and pointed. "Look, there's Léon with your daddy." The square-shaped apartment building had a courtyard in the middle with glass railings. We could see clearly what was happening there from this side.

He elbowed me in the ribs. "Let's get closer."

"...but Léon, I did nothing wrong," the occupant of apartment 85 said. He didn't sound as confident now as he did earlier. I suspected any vampire living in Sterling Meadow had to submit to Léon.

"That's not what we're hearing," Léon said. His tone was deep and throaty, with an edge of warning to his words.

The vampire from apartment 85 was so enormous his frame filled the doorjamb. He reminded me of a demon pro wrestler. He wore low cut dark jeans with no shoes. Sinister tattoos with red flames and naked women filled his chest with more down each arm. His face was smooth and youthful, but that was misleading; the cloud of death surrounding him set off all my alarm bells.

I grabbed Zenon's arm to stop him from getting closer. When he glanced over his shoulder at me, I shook my head. "Don't," I whispered. "Dangerous."

The lines between Zenon's eyes deepened, but he didn't question me. I was serious. Apartment 85 was powerful and even though Léon was there with his brother Sebastian, I feared for their lives.

"There are stories going around about the Mask of Immortality. Do you know where it is?" Léon said, standing straighter, even though he had to crane his head up to see the other demon's face.

Sebastian was bigger than Léon and stronger, but with this demon, I wasn't so sure who would win the fight.

"No, this is the first time I'm hearing about any mask," the vampire demon said, folding his arms across his broad chest and leaned against the doorjamb, feigning boredom.

"Clarke," Léon said his name with so much venom it made my skin crawl. "I've given you a chance. In fact, I've given you many. The information I've received is true, and I'm only here to hear your side of the story. And more importantly, I need to know who you truly work for."

Two men traversed up the stairs and joined Léon and Sebastian. I'd never seen them before and thought they could be their shifter back up; possibly were-leopards from Sebastian's leap.

Clarke pushed away from the doorjamb and stood straight, the muscles in his jaw ticking. "You know I'm a hard worker, Léon, and I've done nothing to anyone. Yes, I work for someone else, but please believe me, if you want to keep this town, you won't ask me again. Because right now, he is already listening to our conversation and he's livid."

Bloody sweat peppered Clarke's forehead as he glanced nervously over his shoulder. Warm wind blew through my hair, and I shivered. Clarke swallowed hard and looked inside his dark apartment again as if someone had arrived.

The darkness that I'd first seen swirling around Clarke's body had dissipated, but it was still there, only now it was farther inside his apartment. Clarke was a vampire, yet he seemed more like a demon from the Underworld; a demon who worked for Victor. Although I'd never seen Clarke in the Underworld before, it was possible he was stationed in Sterling Meadow, being the eyes and ears of the Underworld.

I pinched Zenon's forearm gently. When he glanced down at me, I widened my eyes and mouthed *'dangerous'* again.

A nervousness I didn't feel before washed over me like a cold shower. I glanced over my shoulder as if the dreaded dark shadow was behind me. When I turned to look at Clarke and Léon, the darkness had spread, becoming thicker. Shouting erupted, followed by screaming.

"No! Wait! I said nothing… I swear I said nothing," Clarke screamed to the nothingness inside his apartment. Then the darkness wrapped its tentacles around his neck, shoulders, and waist like an evil octopus and yanked his body inside, slamming the door shut.

Léon, Sebastian, and the two shifters broke the door down and darted inside the apartment. When fighting erupted, Zenon was about to dash off when I grabbed his forearm and shook my head.

"It's not worth it, brother. And besides, you can't die now and here. Not in this time," I said gravely. "We'll find another way to get the answers we seek. I doubt Clarke would've told us, anyway. Léon asked him questions, and he still said nothing. So, as much as I love my father, I'm not risking your life for his."

"Ah," Zenon said. "That's the sweetest thing you've said to me in a long time," he pulled me in for a hug, "now let's get out of here before Léon knows we were close to the action. They are more equipped to sort this out while we wait patiently for them outside."

"Let's use those stairs though," I said, pointing at the other stairs. "I don't feel like bumping into the hungry three downstairs again."

We made it down the stairs while apartment 85 was alive with yelling and fighting. We made it down the stairs unscathed, and just as I was about to open the door after Zenon, when a hand grabbed my right arm.

I yelped in surprise when two glowing red eyes stared

hungrily at me. Before I could call out Zenon's name, the vampire yanked me back inside the building. His friend closed the door, leaning against it, and keeping Zenon outside.

"Well, well, well, she's all alone," hissed the first vampire who had spoken with us. He licked his lips and smiled, revealing his fangs.

"Just leave some for us, Mikey," said his friend.

Mikey pushed me against the door and closed the gap. His blood stench breath assaulted my senses and his dark soul begged for me to play with him. It was a misconception that vampires didn't have souls, because they did. They were the undead. Their hearts had stopped beating and they no longer needed air to breathe, but their souls were still fully intact with their bodies.

So when I grinned at Mikey, his expression changed when I gently pushed my hands into his chest and his soul vibrated a little out of his body. Then when I shoved my palms harder into his chest. Mikey jerked backward as his soul tore halfway out of his body, then popped back in.

"What the fuck was that?" Mikey scowled, shoving me back into the wall beside his friend, my head hitting the hard surface. He kept his hands on my shoulders to keep me in place and squeezed. I cried out in pain, but that seemed to fuel his desire to taste me.

"Much better," Mikey said in a gentle purr, and leaned in. "I love it when human's cry out."

"Luckily I'm not that human," I said, and Mikey cocked his head to one side, his mouth parted in a surprised O while the lines between his eyes deepened.

This time, I gripped his throat and pushed. I screamed as I shoved harder, but Mikey's soul was a stubborn sonofabitch. "Why won't you leave, dammit," I said through gritted teeth.

The more I pushed, the more Mikey leaned into me, snapping his toothy vampire jaw. He stuck his tongue out as if to taste me. Grossed out by his behavior, it fueled my desire to send him to the Underworld in the worst way imaginable. I thought of Dad's power and my hands morphed into talons then back to my human hands. I stifled my smile as I squeezed harder, digging my fingernails into his flesh. His bone snapped as my now powerful fingers pierced his larynx, and his head lulled to one side.

"What the hell?" Mikey stammered, his eyes glaring at me from one side of his neck. "Boys, what is she doing to me?"

"Ah, we got to go," said the other vampires, and I watched them run off in my peripheral vision.

"Seems like they're not good friends," I said sinisterly.

Knocking sounded behind me, with Zenon yelling.

"I'm okay," I yelled. "I'm just sorting this one out quickly." The knocking died down. "Now for you," I said, squeezing Mikey's neck harder, and another bone snapped, pushing his head farther off his shoulder.

Mikey's left eye bulged and stared more to the left as his eyes squinted. His soul edged out of his body and clawed its way back, but I continued pushing.

"You're not a nice vampire, are you, Mikey?" Another bone snapped and Mikey's head was off his shoulder, dangling.

Mikey continued clawing at my shoulders, but he wasn't doing any damage to me. I shoved my fingernails through Mikey's larynx and yanked it out with my right hand while my left hand continued pushing Mikey's soul out of his body.

One part of Victor's power I was grateful for was strength; I wasn't a vampire or a were-animal, but I was my father's child. I had some of his power coursing through my veins, and I used it now to defend myself. My sharp fingernails continued digging into Mikey's neck, tearing his flesh apart. To ensure a vampire was truly dead, his head had to be removed.

Once I tore off Mikey's head, his soul flew out of his body, but before he could return, the Ferryman snapped him up and bolted his soul in his boat. I waved a bloody hand at the Ferryman and smiled.

Mikey's hands let go of my shoulders, then poof, he sparked into a cloud of fire and ash, finally mixing with his blood on the floor.

A loud explosion sounded upstairs, followed by Léon and Sebastian bolting down the stairs. As they came around the corner, they stopped in their tracks, only to find a bloody mess and me in the middle of it.

Léon smiled while Sebastian stared at me like I was a lunatic.

"Hi," I said, waving the same bloodied hand. When a drop of blood fell onto my cheek, I lowered my hand. "Mikey was pestering me," I said, pointing at his blood covered ash on the floor. "He wasn't a nice vampire."

Léon chuckled. "No, Mikey was one of our troublemakers. Thank you for doing us a service. I owe you one." He winked wickedly and grinned.

"How did it go?" I asked, opening the door to find Zenon standing there with his arms folded over his chest and a surprised look on his face when he saw me covered in blood.

"Unfortunately, we don't know who had sent Clarke, but we know it's a demon. They destroyed Clarke before we could ask more questions. So, whoever it was doing this was there in the Underworld. You should ask Victor more questions about this. He may have heard something down there while you've been away."

"Thanks, Léon, we appreciate your help," I said, pulling a wet wipe out of my bag to clean my hands. It was times like these when I wished I had my gloves. The adrenaline was wearing off and my stomach turned. I swallowed the bile in my throat and shuddered.

"Any time," Léon said, closing the gap. Before I could exit, Léon turned to me, blocking me from leaving. "How do I meet your mother?" he whispered near the shell of my left ear, ensuring nobody else had heard. When he came into my vision once more, his blue eyes were swimming in curiosity.

I grabbed his left shoulder and leaned in near his left ear and whispered how they met and what he and Sebastian did to save her life.

Léon beamed with pride and nodded in satisfaction. He glanced at Sebastian, who shrugged; the desperation on his face needing to know what he and I had spoken about, but I doubted Léon would ever tell him.

"I guess we'll see you two in the future," Léon said, holding the door open for me.

As Zenon and I traversed down the stairs and onto the sidewalk, Sebastian asked who we were and what our discussion was about. I grinned when Léon nonchalantly told him it was none of his business. Brothers…

Chapter Eighteen

I grabbed Zenon's hand, but the moment we touched, he transported us straight back to the secret tomb before I could think about breathing. It was so sudden and unexpected that when we landed at the bottom of the building near that same tree, I tripped, almost hitting a branch with my face.

"Jeez, brother, easy tiger," I said, pressing my hands against the branch to stay upright. A flurry of butterflies fluttered inside my stomach while a swarm of bees erupted inside my skull. I gagged when nausea flooded my stomach and shuddered when bile rose in my throat.

"Are you okay?" Zenon asked, patting my back when I doubled over.

"Couldn't you have waited for me to at least say when I was ready?"

"What?" He shrugged. "I thought you were used to it?"

"I was. I am." I swallowed hard. "It happened so quickly you took me by surprise."

Zenon's gaze raked over my body with his cool, yellow

eyes and arched an eyebrow for effect. "You've never been this ill before, and I always teleport quickly. That's what you loved about teleporting with me."

"I know," I said, still hunched over and coughing into my hand. When I could breathe properly, I stood straight and rounded my shoulders. I pushed some hair out of my face and wiped my mouth dry.

"Are you ready?" Zenon asked when he reached the top of the stairs.

"And why are we out here instead of inside?" I asked, slowly climbing the stairs. "The last few times we've teleported directly inside the secret tomb."

"I pictured the tomb in my mind's eye, but alas, this was where it brought us." Zenon pushed open the main door and entered, not bothering to wait for me. "Hurry," he said sternly.

I ran up the last couple of steps and pushed the door open and smacked straight into Zenon's back. "What…" I mumbled, rubbing my nose.

"Shush," Zenon whispered, grabbing a hold of my arm to keep me behind his back.

I grabbed his upper arms to stabilize myself and peered around his right side. I flinched when I saw the beast and for a moment everything went quiet, as if my heart had stopped. There in the far corner of the entrance stood a strange creature hunched over, trying to open the door to the secret tomb; but it only had two thumbs on each hand. It stood on muscular goat's legs with a red cloth slung over its large, muscular back.

Zenon stepped backward, pushing me outside. My foot kicked a pebble, sending it clanking across the floor. I gripped Zenon's arms in anticipation. We froze.

The creature stopped doing what it was doing and stood

up, doubling in size. Slowly, it turned around to find the object of the noise—us—and another pair of arms unfolded from behind its back. It stared hungrily at us with glowing red eyes, spittle running down its toothy jaw and flaring its nostrils.

"What is it?" I whispered, staring at the strange man-goat-like-creature.

The demon had long black hair that would make most women jealous except for the two sets of curved horns protruding from the sides of its head. Its double pixie ears moved, listening. It grunted, sending plumes of smoke out of its nostrils. "Open," it said, pointing a thumb at the door.

I swallowed my laugh and hid behind Zenon who shook me off his shoulders and approached the demon.

"Who are you?" Zenon asked carefully, closing the gap with the demon-goat.

The demon-goat grunted again, forcing Zenon to stop, and he raised both hands in surrender. The demon-goat kicked up a cloven hoof, sending dust everywhere. "Open!" It yelled, still pointing at the door.

"Okay," Zenon said. "We mean you no harm. I'll open the door and then you tell us how you got here and why you're here?" He pointed at the door, silently asking the demon-goat permission to move, and the demon nodded. Zenon approached the demon cautiously, with me trailing closely behind him. If the demon were to attack us, he'd grab Zenon first, while I could help if he needed me. The best defense was to use a sibling as a shield. I grinned at the I'm-a-terrible-sister-thought but squashed it immediately. I'd never let my brother get hurt if I could help.

When we reached the door to the secret tomb, the demon-goat stepped away from us, and plumes of smoke continued coming out of its nostrils. I narrowed my eyes at the creature but kept Zenon between us.

"Are you from the Underworld?" I asked the demon. The short walk from the main entrance to this door, the demon kept its eyes on Zenon, but when I spoke, its eyes flitted from him to me, and they glowed redder.

The demon-goat nodded its head in affirmation, then its eyes flitted back to Zenon. Knowing that Victor was down in the Underworld while a creature was here now was too coincidental. If there was anything I'd learned from Dad was that nothing was as it seemed. Someone had sent the demon-goat here, but why. Was it sent here to fetch the mask?

Another puff of smoke came out of its nostrils and its second pair of arms folded across its large gray chest with glowing red tattoos. From a distance, its tattoos just seemed like red paint, but up close, the glowing red tattoos moved like a five-second clip. Thin waves of steam oozed out of its pores and at this closeness to the creature, I felt heat beat against me, making me sweat like I was in a sauna.

The more involved we became in Victor's dilemma, the more I realized it related to the Underworld. There were too many instances that pointed to the Underworld; the Mask of Immortality, the reptiles who killed Alec, the magician and his assistant, and now this demon-goat, all connected to the Underworld. I just didn't understand how, who, or why. There had to be something else at play here.

Zenon pushed open the door to the tomb and a wave of heat smacked us in the face, pushing him into me and I almost flew backward if I wasn't still holding onto his shirt. Dust particles danced in the air, which I tried waving away, but they remained suspended near our faces as if frozen in time.

I entered the tomb first but didn't get farther than the doorjamb. Everything within the tomb had frozen, with no air to breathe. It was strange at first to comprehend what I was seeing, but the more I stared at the room, the more confused I became. River sat motionless with the dust particles surrounding him. I cocked my head to the side and squinted. The sarcophagus was closed again and doubted River had the energy to do that, but I had no answer how he could've done it himself or why.

I glanced over my shoulder to tell Zenon something strange was going on, but that room had winked out into the darkness. My brother blended in with the shadows and the demon-goat with him.

I blinked and turned to face River when he, too, disappeared.

I gripped the satchel strap tightly in my fist and pulled my knife out from behind my back. The air whipped my cheek, pushing me against the doorjamb; at least this way I had a view of the darkening main entrance and the secret tomb.

Screams sounded from both rooms as everything darkened. The demon we'd seen earlier materialized once more and reached for me.

Chapter Nineteen

"It's okay, I've got you," said someone behind me with a sensual baritone that made all the hairs on my body stand on end.

I tried using my knife on him, but he had pinned my arms to my sides with his muscular arms. I opened my eyes to darkness, blinking vigorously until my eyes adjusted to the gloomy light.

The cavernous room was dark save for the torches that floated in the air. The walls moved with what looked like streams of water running upward instead of downward. And on one side of the room was a neatly made bed and a chest of drawers, and on the other side, a maroon couch. The last thing I expected was to land in someone's bedroom and struggled against his tightening grip.

"Easy princess," he said against my head, sending another wave of sensual pleasure throughout my body. "I'm not the enemy," he grunted, squeezing harder, taking my breath away.

When I moaned in pain, he slowly loosened his grip. "I

won't hurt you, I promise. My name is Osmodeus, or Os for short," Os said, still holding tight. "Now, do you promise not to stab me with that huge knife in your hands when I let you go. This isn't the type of foreplay I'm into," he said with a chuckle.

I nodded, trying not to think of his naked body pressed up against mine. "Just let go," I breathed, as I stopped struggling against him. I exhaled and relaxed my body.

A purple tail came into my peripheral vision as the demon slowly let go of me. "Now no sudden movements. I'd hate to knock you out." He helped me stand on my own and without swaying.

"What happened, and who are you?" I asked, turning around to look at the demon, the lines between my eyes deepening.

"Take all the time you need," Os said, stepping away from me, wearing a salacious smile. His dark gaze raked up and down my body like I was food. Then my body betrayed me by responding to his temptation.

I scowled, making Os laugh. The purple demon stood almost six feet tall, very muscular, with black eyes and pointy horns protruding out of his head. When he smiled, his sharp teeth left me on edge because I knew those teeth could easily rip me apart.

I rounded my shoulders and sheathed my knife. I clutched the satchel against my body, but when there was nothing slung against my body, I panicked.

"Is this what you're looking for?" Os said, holding up my satchel.

"Give that back," I said, reaching for it.

Os pressed his palm against my face and kept the satchel out of my reach. "Easy there princess—"

"I'm not a princess," I growled.

"Are you sure about that?" he said, arching a purple eyebrow. "I'll give this back if you tell me what you are doing here?"

"Well, for one, I don't know where here is?" I said, sounding annoyed, and pointed at the bed. "I take it this is your humble abode?"

"Yes, and the last time a human fell into my room, she bound herself to me. But I don't see that happening now," he said, staring at me from my head to my toes, "so I ask again, what are you doing here?"

"I'd love to know. I don't even know who you are," I grumbled. "But it has to be the Underworld?"

Os nodded.

"I told you why I was here now. Please give that back," I said, reaching for my satchel.

"Fine," he grumbled and handed it back.

"Did you see my brother? Tall guy with yellow eyes?"

"Nope, you're the only thing I've seen all day. I was about to go back to the human world for a midnight snack with my lady friend when you fell into my lap like a present from the gods." He chuckled.

I groaned when I noticed his growing erection. He was purple, a demon, and provided sensual pleasure.

"That's right honey, incubus at your service." His grin was like an aphrodisiac and could set a woman's panties on fire, but luckily, I had my father's power and extinguished it like cold water. Os frowned as if sensing what I'd done. "What are you?" he said, walking around me. "You are no plain human female, although you look the part and almost smell the part. No, you are not like them at all... you are, however, something most delicious and I want a taste." He snapped his toothy jaw at me.

I snorted. As much as I tried to be ladylike around new

people, every now and then, my defenses slipped, and my laugh sounded like a snort.

"Let's just say I can block wiles of vampires and incubi."

"Then why are you here?"

"I'd like to know the same thing. One moment I was with Zenon in the secret tomb, the next moment the strange demon-goat grinned, and everything went black and I landed on top of you."

"Demon-goat?" Os said, clearly confused.

"Yes, he had cloven hooves. His muscular upper body looked similar to a man with double arms and hot red tattoos that moved, and steam coming out of his pores."

Os's expression changed from confusion to knowing exactly what I was referring to.

"Secret tomb, you say?"

I nodded.

"Shit," he said, rushing past me. "Come, princess, we have to go."

"Wait, what do you mean? What's going on?"

"We can walk and talk," he said, opening a wooden door at the far end of his room. "I think I know what's going on, but my brother will know more."

"Who is your brother?"

"Osmodos, or Ossie."

"Are you twins?"

"No, Osmodos is my older and apparently wiser brother," Os grunted as we traversed the hallways of the Underworld. "It's only because he reads words all day, every day. Sometimes he performs spells and uses his magic for good—"

"And he's a demon?" I'd never heard of any demon using magic for good. If there was a decent demon out there, I wanted to know more about him.

"Yeah, I know. It doesn't happen often, but I promise you we are good demons," Os smiled, glancing over his shoulder and winked wickedly. "It's a pity it doesn't work on you, or you'd be dripping in your juices by now."

"Thank goodness it doesn't work," I grumbled, then almost slammed into his back.

"We're here," he said, standing near a portal.

I groaned when I saw the shimmering doorway. "Where does this go?" I asked, not impressed, and not wanting nausea to flood my system again. And I didn't know we had portals within the Underworld, but then again, I didn't know everything there was to know about my father's world.

"It will take us directly to my brother's library."

Os held out his hand for me to take, and the moment I did, I caught glimpses of images. He had changed form and was human, with blond hair, and was gorgeous. He was helping a woman, and another man—

Os cleared his throat, cutting the vision short. "No spying on my life, princess. Those memories are mine."

"Sorry, I didn't know I could do that," I said, staring at the hand that held Os's, not believing I could see someone else's memories like that. It had never happened to me before. "Who were those people?" I asked, wanting to understand more about what I saw.

"Me and my brother helped a female escape this place and her terrible situation in the city. It happened a while ago. But we can't talk about it now. Let's go."

I nodded, grabbing Os's hand once more and walked with him through the portal. This time, I saw no memories but sparkly darkness, and I experienced no nausea. We entered through the doorway and into the largest library I'd ever seen. There were rows and rows of shelves filled with large tomes. The library was so big I couldn't see the end of the rows; they continued on and on.

The library was beautiful, with intricate carvings stained with gold on the wooden bookshelves. Adorned on the cream-colored walls were golden torches that created the perfect lighting. The air smelled fresh with a gentle under-tone of bibliosmia. This place was nothing like my father's rooms or any library in my world.

"Wow," I said, marveling at the place. "It's stunning." The large glass chandeliers hanging from the ceiling brought an ambiance to the place like no other.

"Yes, yes, an educated woman's wet dream. Just don't fall for my brother. He's a complete nerd for a Demon Lord—"

"He's a Demon Lord? Are you?" I asked, almost running to keep up with him.

"See, I just mention this, and you're practically drool-ing," he said with a sly smirk.

I rolled my eyes.

"Anyway, as I was saying before you rudely interrupted me," he said seriously, but smiled. "He loves this place; it's his home. He maintains order within the Underworld Library, and he keeps the tomes safe. He is the keeper of information, and nobody can lie to him. It's quite a gift if you ask me. And if anybody removes a tome, he makes sure they returned them swiftly—or he won't blink twice to remove fingers, arms, legs, and even heads."

My eyes widened at that, and Os chuckled.

"But only if they deserve it."

"Naturally," I said, agreeing but secretly afraid of what both demons could do to me. "Is he also an incubus?"

"No, just a very scary and very powerful demon."

"Where does he keep the important tomes?" I asked as

we traversed down the main row of the elegant library. My eyes bounced around the large room, taking it all in. I'd love to sit here and read.

"Ha, like I would tell you. But Osmodos keeps the important tomes on shelves locked behind secret doors, and he is the only one with a key."

I nodded. I didn't blame him. If I worked here, I'd do the same thing. "What are the tomes about?" Victor never shared with me the details of any room inside the Underworld. Knowing that there was a library filled with so much information was a treasure.

"Everything and anything. It explains all you need to know about demons, angels, vampires, were-animals, fairies, etcetera. All events that have happened before and after. Some tomes hold the future… but that one nobody has opened. Not even Ossie."

That caught my attention, and I stared open-mouthed at Os.

"Close that, princess, before I put something inside for you to suck."

I promptly closed my mouth and fought not to smile. He was a pervert, but at least he was funny.

"Now where is that blasted brother of mine. Ossie!" Os yelled.

"Must you always yell, brother?" Ossie said, coming into view a few rows away.

I stopped dead in my tracks. My mouth hanging open as I stared up at Ossie. Although I didn't know the extent of Ossie's power, I sensed how great it was. The air surrounding him pulsed with electricity and the hairs on my arms pebbled.

His powerful black/metallic scales rippled in the dim light. His horns were large and pointy, and his eyes were as black as night. He stood almost double my size, and all I did was gawk up at him. All the years I'd been alive, I'd never seen someone as dangerously beautiful as him. My father was powerful, but Ossie was something else.

Ossie sensed my uneasiness and morphed into a more appealing human form. He slunk down to size and had long, silky black hair tied in a ponytail, bright green eyes, and a charming smile.

"Not again," Ossie said. "I swear I promised nobody. Whoever this female is, she isn't mine."

"Haha, no, it's not that. This is," Os said, staring at me. "What's your name, luv?"

I licked dry lips but never glanced away from Ossie. "Ah," I mumbled, forgetting my name. "Scout, my name is Scout."

"Shit," Ossie said. His eyes flitting between Os and me. "You're Victor's daughter, aren't you?"

"Dammit," Os said, standing farther away from me. "What have you done, luv?" he said to me.

115

Chapter Twenty

"I did nothing. I'm only…" I left my sentence hanging because Victor had said not to tell anyone. Nobody could know I was his daughter or that he was gravely ill. Yet these demon brothers already knew about me, and who my father was. This left me with an uneasy feeling.

"Well, what is it?" Ossie said. His green eyes held secrets I wish I knew.

I stepped closer to Ossie, my mouth still dry. "Is there water here or maybe something stronger?" I stared at Ossie in desperation. I didn't think water would help settle my nerves and hoped he had something potent like absinthe and I could hallucinate my way out of this mess.

"Come," Ossie said, walking away from me. "I'm sure there's an old Scotch Whiskey or something you could down. You look a little disheveled. Are you joining us, brother?"

"You know this is silly. She's like a myth they warned us never to find. Yet she literally fell into my arms."

"Don't be a baby. Now come."

I followed Ossie right to the other side of the library, stopping near a blazing fireplace with a liquor cabinet nearby. He poured us each a glass, handing me the one with the most. I thanked him and downed the honey-whiskey he offered and asked for another one.

When I glanced back at Os, he took the drink from his brother and downed it, too. I did a double take because he had morphed into his human form, but his purple tail continued swishing behind him like an agitated cat. He had shaved dark brown hair on the sides of his head, but it was long and neat on top. His blue eyes reminded me of the color of tropical blue and his skin dark like he'd just had a tan. He had a week's worth of stubble on his jaw and a kind smile. I blinked at him. He reminded me of River.

River...

I hoped he was okay. We had our disagreements in the past, and I was still a little mad at him, but wanted no harm to come to him. I only wanted the best for him, despite our past. But he had looked sickly earlier before he too had disappeared.

And father...

Father was hanging on by a thread. I needed to find the mask—

A glass came into my view, pulling me back into the present. I smiled sadly, took the glass from Ossie, and enjoyed a smaller sip. The first glass of whiskey I'd downed did its job, easing my anxiety and shaky nerves. When I looked from Ossie to Os, I flinched. Os had changed again and now had amber-brown-colored eyes; almost exactly like River's.

"What did you just do?"

"You like?"

"Yes, no, I mean yes. It's freaky."

"No, it's not. I project what women want, and in this case, this is what you want. Is it not?" Os said, flaunting his half-naked body.

"Yes, I mean no... I just thought of someone and then you..." I pointed at Os, "look like this. I could think of a dead friend, and you do that and remind me of him. Do you want me sad?"

"No," Os said defensively. "I didn't mean to. Is your friend dead?" Os's features changed again to green eyes and blond hair, but the boyish good looks remained.

"He isn't dead... well, not yet." I sighed, having another sip.

"Good, because I prefer the darker look." Os changed back to River's amber-brown colored eyes, brown hair, and dark stubble along his jawline.

When I glanced at Ossie, he smiled kindly, and I smiled sheepishly. I downed the rest of the drink and placed the glass on the table with a shudder. Whiskey had that honey-burning-liquid that could help one throw up if downed too quickly.

I waited for the demon-brothers to finish their drinks before saying anything else. I needed more information. There had to be a reason the secret tomb had sent me to them instead of disappearing with that demon-goat and Zenon.

I flinched again when a couch that wasn't there before appeared and the burning fireplace floated mid-air and closer. I raised my chilly hands toward the warm fire that reminded me of the Eternal Fire.

Once my bones had thawed, I sat on the couch with a loud sigh and leaned back on the soft cushion. My muscles seemed to melt into the comfortable couch, and then my joints began to ache.

I didn't know how long I'd been up and about, but it felt like a week without eating or sleeping. I wanted to ask the demon brother's questions, but I closed my eyes. Movement to my right caught me off guard and I bolted upright, but it was only the brothers who had neared.

"It's okay, tiny human princess," Ossie said, sitting beside me. "You're safe with us."

Chapter Twenty-One

I closed my eyes for just a second and I drifted off into the sky with a sparkling blue ocean below, and a thick wall of ice surrounding it. The sun was warm against my chilled body, and I smiled. The smell of rose petals wafted in the air, and I could dance in the sky forever. A dark maze came into focus and I blinked the vision away. I landed with a thud inside Victor's room, and I remembered he was dying. I awoke with a start and bolted upright in a panic. Ossie stood beside me and pulled me back down to sit next to him again.

"Easy, Scout," Ossie whispered gently. His left arm was around my shoulders, cradling me against his warm body. I nestled into his safety, feeling grateful for the compassion. "You were only asleep for five minutes, and besides, time is different in the library, so there's no need to rush off anywhere."

"Like it is in the Underworld?" I asked, sitting up and turning my body toward him with my right leg bent and on the couch.

"No," Ossie said, glancing nervously at Os, then back at me, "time stands completely still here. Here," he waved his hands in the air, "there is no time. Now, tell Uncle Os and me what's going on."

I narrowed my eyes at the demon brothers. "How do I know I can trust you?" Victor was explicit. I wasn't to share anything with anyone, and especially not demon's even though they were good and kind and brothers.

"Luv, there's a reason they sent you to us," Os said, glancing just as nervously at his brother. "We are not like your usual demons."

"What does that mean?" I asked, my eyes narrowing suspiciously at them.

Ossie touched my hand, and we shared a blue spark between us. This was something only Victor and I could do; it first happened after my initiation quest. We had raised our hands together without touching and the blue electricity ran between us. I raised my hand in unison with Ossie and Os, and the brothers did the same. I watched in delight as the blue spark glowed between us three, joining us.

"Am I correct in saying you are Victor's daughter?" Ossie asked, lowering his hand and the blue spark between us disappeared; but it remained between Os and me until I lowered my hand.

I nodded. "Yes, and Blaire Thorne is my mother." The demon brothers shared another nervous glance that just irritated me. "Okay, what is going on. You two are strange demons, and I demand to know." I pointed from one brother to the other. "You keep sharing these looks. Now tell me."

"We have to tell her," Os said, pulling a chair closer to me.

The fireplace continued burning, warming the area, and

it felt like home away from home. Adorned on the walls, the torches burned brightly, setting the idyllic scene. The smell of books assaulted my nose, but in a good way, and I sat between the demon brothers, which should have caused concern, but it didn't. They didn't scare me and I felt oddly at peace between them.

"You can never repeat what we are about to tell you," Ossie said seriously. "If anyone found out, it could be the end of all of us."

"Yes, fine. Now what is it?" I grumbled, folding my arms across my chest.

"Victor—"

"Is ill, I know," I said, interrupting Ossie.

"What?" Os said. "No, that's not what my brother was going to say."

"Oh, sorry, please continue." I bit my lip, cursing myself for letting it slip.

"What do you mean he is ill?" Ossie asked.

"Never mind, you carry on."

"Scout, tell us," Os demanded, his horns showing slightly. "If Victor is ill, we need to know what happened. We can help."

I sighed, feeling like an idiot for saying Father was ill, but from the way the brothers spoke, it sounded like they already knew that. Unfortunately, they didn't know and now they wanted to know the details. I didn't know if I could trust them, and for some strange reason I thought I could, I had to tell them. Perhaps they knew things I didn't and they could help.

"Someone used the Mask of Immortality on him and we have been trying to find it to reverse what had happened to him. River and I ended up in the secret tomb and then we called my brother Zenon to help us. We seemed to have been able to jump timelines and when we got back, River had fallen ill and now he and Zenon are missing. We know a demon is behind everything, but we don't know who." I narrowed my eyes at the brothers. "Maybe it's you two."

"Don't be ridiculous. What else can you tell us? Where is Victor now?" Ossie peppered me with questions, his interest piqued.

"That's just it," I said wearily. "We went back to the secret tomb, and we came across that goat-like-demon and then everything went black, and I landed in Os's lap. I don't know what happened to River or Zenon and now I'm hoping either of you can help figure this out." I sat back, out of breath.

The demon brothers stared nervously at each other.

I flinched when Ossie jumped up and bolted toward a picture on the far wall. Against the wall stood shelves coated in gold engravings and, depending how the light struck it, it was almost too bright to look at.

Os stood up and reached for me. I took the hand he proffered, and we joined Ossie near those exquisite golden bookcases. He pulled on a torch on the wall, revealing a hidden door. It amazed me he did this in front of me. He knew nothing about me yet trusted me enough to show me this hidden room.

I glanced up at Ossie, smiling, but he was concentrating on the secret door.

"This, my dear, is the real Secret Tomb," Ossie said, descending the stairs into the room. "That tomb you're referring to is a time portal that will continue looping if you don't know what you're doing. You'll go back to the future, to the present, to the past, until you're blue in the face. One good thing about that tomb is time didn't move for you or Victor. It's as if you just left him. You also won't age but this," he raised his arms up in worship, "this is the real Secret Tomb."

I followed Ossie down the stairs and into the large tomb that was filled with old tomes, portraits, jewels, and swords. All the hairs on my body stood on end and I shivered from the cold, but there were no air vents here. The room felt like a cement safe guarded by magic.

I glanced around the room at each item and my mouth opened in a surprise *O*; they each glowed in different colors, which I assumed was the type of magic used to keep it safe. I raised my hand to touch a golden chalice, but Os smacked my hand away and shook his head.

"Yes, that's correct," Ossie said, as if reading my mind. His dark scales moved beneath his human skin, reminding me of Victor's armor. "Each item is guarded by different types of magic, and I wouldn't touch any of them if I were you."

"You read minds?"

"A little, but that thought of yours was so loud it's like you were screaming it. I'm sure even Os heard you." Ossie smiled, and I beamed up at him. "This," Ossie continued, opening a large tome, "will give us all the information we need to help Victor. And that Mask of Immortality is dangerous, but I know how to locate it. If there's a demon within the Underworld who has it," he glanced at Os with a raised eyebrow, "we'll be able to retrieve it and help Victor."

For a moment I had felt lost and hopeless as my father laid dying in his room. Now, as my eyes filled with tears, my heart filled with hope. I silently thanked the stars and the other secret time tomb for bringing me to the demon brothers. With their knowledge, I now believed we could sort this out before Victor and River ran out of time.

Ossie ran his fingers over the pages. Page after page he

read and read, but all I heard were mumbles. He read so fast I couldn't keep up. The words on the pages were not English or Latin, but script I'd never seen or heard before. It was a demon language I didn't understand.

"You might as well sit down," Os said, pulling up a chair and sitting down. "This will take a while."

"Can you read these books?"

"Me?" Os laughed. "Heavens no. This is all Ossie's territory. I'm more the love demon than the word demon." His grin was contagious, and I smiled at him, sitting down beside him.

We waited in silence while Ossie read through that book, and I took the time to take in my surroundings. When I'd first entered the real Secret Tomb, the force of magic was so heavy it took me back a bit, but the longer I stayed inside the room, the more it spoke to me. The more I felt the raw magic behind it, but more importantly, how old the magic was, and it left me feeling nervous.

The demon brothers were each powerful in their own way, but then so was I. My little black wings fluttered behind me, and I pushed them back. I didn't want the brothers seeing them and laughing. I still had to get my larger wings and until then I'd keep them hidden, and would wait in silence until Ossie finished.

Chapter Twenty-Two

Victor sat on his bed, unable to move. Dark shadows moved across the wall, painting him in darkness. The smell of wet dirt assaulted my nose, and a chill in the air forced me to hug myself. The figure on the bed did not look like my father. He stared at me with dark sunken eyes, and his gaunt face scared me. His armor no longer shined, and his long dark hair was white. I was running out of time. If I didn't find the Mask of Immortality soon, I'd lose him and River forever.

"Does she know?" A female said in the distance.

I squinted in the bright light, raising my hands to shield my face, but I saw only white light.

"We haven't gotten to that yet," Os said, still sitting beside me.

My eyes flittered open, and I bolted upright. I gripped the sides of the chair, relieved I didn't fall off it. Glancing around the room, it relieved me we were still inside the Secret Tomb with all the magical glowing artifacts. Ossie

126

was still reading the same tome and beside me sat Os, with an unknown woman. They stared at me.

"What?" I asked, combing my fingers through my long hair. "Was I drooling?" I wiped my mouth.

"No, luv," Os said, smiling. "But I do want to introduce you to my Julia," he said, pointing at the woman beside him. She had light brown hair, blue eyes, and a dimple in one cheek when she smiled. "She's my significant other."

"You," I pointed at Os and then Julia, "are mated? You," I pointed at Os again, "mated with a human?"

"Don't look so surprised. Incubi can mate, you know." Os almost sounded insulted. "And humans are the best kind of mate." He grinned lovingly at Julia.

"No, it's not that. It's just I've never heard of that before. Congratulations," I said, trying to sound happy, but my thoughts kept going back to Victor and how awful he looked in my vision. "Is that the woman I saw flashes of when I touched your hand?"

"Yes," Os said, beaming. "This is she. What a whirlwind that was," he pulled her closer to his side and kissed the top of her head, "I think we rescued each other that day. And it all worked out in the end."

"It's a pleasure to meet you, Scout. I've heard a lot about you," Julia said. I opened my mouth to ask what had she heard when she raised her hand, shushing me. "All good, I promise, and only the important stuff," she said, smiling kindly. Her face was way too angelic to be in the company of a sexual demon, but who was I to judge. I loved a walking ball of flames who did my father's contract work; I couldn't point fingers.

"Ossie, have you got any info for us yet?" I asked, stifling a yawn and rubbing my eyes.

Ossie turned around to answer me, but the expression he wore said little. "We need to find Victor."

"He's in his room."

Ossie shook his head. "No, he isn't."

I sat upright. "No, he is," I said, convincingly. "River and I left him there ourselves. And I... I just saw him there in my dream."

Ossie shook his head and opened his palm where a red orb glowed, showing Victor sitting on a bed I'd never seen before.

"Where is that?"

Ossie's eyes flitted to Os. "Let's use Caesar. He'll be able to sniff out his owner." Caesar was my father's three-heads-one-body spirit animal. I could kick myself for not thinking of using him first.

"My father warned me not to approach Caesar without him." I glanced nervously at the demon brothers. "You know what he's capable of."

"We know, princess, but you forget, we're demons from the Underworld," Ossie said, heading for the exit. "Come on, we don't have all day." As Ossie exited the Secret Tomb, his human form enlarged, and he morphed back into his deadly demon form. His black scales shimmering in the dim light as he walked across the shiny tiles of the library.

"I'll bring lunch," Os said, grabbing hold of Julia's hand and running after Ossie.

Not wanting to be left alone in the Underworld Library, I followed the brothers to the far right-hand side where a shimmering doorway stood waiting. I frowned, not remembering this doorway earlier, but so much had happened lately, I was sure my brain was just protecting me.

Ossie waited for me to catch up and held out his hand. "It's just easier holding on to one of us. If you don't know where you're going, you'll end up in one of the Chambers of Hell. Not a pretty sight for a pretty girl like you. If you know what I'm saying?"

Blood drained from my face and I nodded, quickly reaching for his hand; it was soft, and he was gentle holding mine, and we walked through the shimmering doorway together. The change in space and time felt like walking through clouds, and my stomach didn't threaten to turn on me. We stepped out into Caesar's lair, where we stood in the darkness and waited. My eyes adjusted to the gloomy room, and nails scratching on the floor made the hairs at the back of my neck stand up. But when a puppy ran up to me, I smiled.

Caesar sniffed and licked my hand, each head taking turns getting scratched behind the ears. They wore a large collar around their thick neck, which was connected to a chain on the wall. Vic had said the collar and chain shouldn't fool me because Caesar would break it easily if he felt threatened.

"Caesar," Ossie said, crouching near the animal. Caesar stopped licking my hands and sat down, staring up at Ossie like a good doggie. "Victor is missing, and we need your help." Caesar growled and started growing. "Easy puppy," Ossie said, scratching Caesar behind the first dog's ear. "We need your help in locating him. Do you think you can do that for us?"

Caesar nodded and licked Ossie's hand.

I stood watching this exchange and found it strange Caesar didn't find the brothers intimidating or threatening. I'd seen other demons walk past Caesar's lair and get mauled to dust. Yet he was comfortable with them and myself included, without Victor having been here.

It made me wonder whether Vic was right about Caesar

wanting to hurt me or if he just wanted to scare me so that I didn't walk around the Underworld alone. There were so many passageways, secret doors, hidden levels I could easily get lost in. I'd been around so often Caesar must've gotten used to me being here. It relieved me, but I wouldn't test Caesar; he was a demon beast and extremely dangerous.

Ossie placed the piece of steak Os had nabbed from somewhere in front of Caesar. Each head gobbled up his share and then they started growing into the large, scary beast that would give anyone nightmares.

Caesar stood almost as tall as Ossie in his demon-dog form. The collar had broken off and laid on the floor near their paws, while their eyes had bled from black to silver, their teeth razor sharp, and their mouths salivated. Their fur was no longer soft and fluffy, but matted and short. Their paws had also grown talons sharp enough to slice my body into pieces.

I stepped backward until I bumped into the wall. Pressing my palms against the icy surface, I flinched when something slimy brushed up against my palms and back. Quickly, I stepped forward again. I'd forgotten Vic's other warning, never touch the walls. I glanced over my shoulder and found a face trying to push its way through the wall. Its tongue licking up the inside of the wall and I cringed, realizing the tongue had most likely licked me. The torches adorned on the walls were of the gargoyle pained faces, and they all faced me, screaming silently.

A nervousness swept through me, and I ran away from the wall, bumping into something hard yet furry. I froze, unsure what Caesar would do. Slowly, I turned around and glanced up at Caesar's front paw, and I waited for them to bite my head off. Instead, the head closest to me licked my face, wetting my hair.

Ossie reached for my hand and pulled me to his side. "I think it's best to stand here by me before they lick you everywhere," Ossie said with a smirk. "Are you ready, boys?" he said to Caesar. "Find your master and we're right behind you."

Caesar growled, each head unhappy that their owner was missing, and they took off at a dangerously fast pace while I ran human slow. Ossie realized I'd fallen behind, waited for me and grabbed hold of my waist, turning his body slightly so that I could easily climb onto his back. I clung to his thick scaly neck like a bushbaby and together we chased after the beast.

Chapter Twenty-Three

Ossie ran so fast behind Caesar the world blurred past. Tears streamed down my face, forcing me to press my head against his back while I clung to him. We passed various areas that went from hot to cold to warm again. I didn't know all the levels of the Underworld and hoped the demon brothers and Caesar would take care of me in Vic's absence.

Finally, we stopped. Wiping my eyes dry, I could see again. I peered around Ossie's large scaly black shoulder when Caesar started barking. We stood outside a closed wooden door with wrought iron hinges and delicate vine engravings on the door that glowed like the door was breathing.

Os and Julia were in their purple demon form, their tails swishing left and right in unison. Their dark talons were up and out, ready to fight anything behind the door.

I did a second glance at Julia, who did nothing but glance my way. Her purple body was beautiful and curvy in all the right places. She seemed to glow in a dim light that hid nothing, and being a succubus, she was extremely attractive, and I felt myself drawn to her like a moth to a flame.

When Os pulled Julia to stand on his other side, the connection we shared shattered like glass on the floor. I shivered from the loss of warmth and my cheeks heated.

Ossie pushed past everyone, helping me off his back, and opened the door.

Not wanting to be caught in Julia's magnetism again, I stood beside Caesar, who had shrunk down to normal dog size, and scratched behind their ears. "Who's a good doggie? You're good doggies… yes, you are," I said, rubbing one head after the other. Their shared tail slapping hard against the floor in happiness as their tongues fell out of their mouths. "Such good floofs," I whispered. "I hope our father is here and safe." The middle head yelped and licked my face. I saw in their dark eyes they were worried about our father too.

The door squeaked open, and Ossie entered. A cool sea breeze whipped my face, and I followed him. Caesar walked beside me while the two sexy purple demons followed close behind.

The world beyond the wooden door was breathtakingly stunning. I stood with my mouth wide open. I knew the Underworld had worlds within the larger realm and among them hidden gems, but this world was something else. It was an ocean filled with majestic creatures; dolphins with different shaped noses, seahorses the size of ponies and of various colors never seen before, and a variety of fish I didn't know the names to.

I held my breath, so that I didn't drown, and stepped inside. But… I frowned when cool air brushed against my face. I exhaled and inhaled. I touched Ossie's back, and he glanced over his shoulder down at me; plumes of smoke coming out of his nostrils and his metallic black eyes sparkled.

"What's wrong?" he asked, his tone deep and throaty.

"I can breathe here?" I said, shrugging. "How can we be under water?" I breathed in for additional effect and a school of fish swam past, darting left then right as they followed the leader.

Ossie stopped walking, and I almost bumped into the back of him. "Victor has told you about the various worlds within the Underworld?" I nodded. "Well, each world holds creatures specific to their world or realm. Therefore, if they kill a good mermaid, their souls come to this ocean. While those evil mermaids get taken somewhere, not as nice." He raised his claws and a star fish bounced off the tip of his one talon. "It's fascinating once you have seen all the levels." He smiled as his metallic scales glistened in the ocean light.

"I knew there was more to the Underworld than I realized, but never could I imagine an ocean within, and I could breathe underwater."

Ossie thought for a moment, then spoke, "It's not so much as you breathing underwater, but the water giving way to you in order to breathe. Does that make sense?"

"It does," I said, and my eyes flitted to the side when a dark shadow emerged from the depths of the seafloor. I pushed Ossie to the side and pointed. He grabbed my hand and lowered it.

"Never point at the Queen of the Seven Seas," he whispered so only I could hear, but his lips barely moved. The dark figure neared, stopping in front of us. "My Queen," he said, letting go of my hand.

The Queen of the Seven Seas floated closer. I couldn't

see her clearly at first since seaweed floated around her, but the closer she came, I had to do a double take.

Her hair moved like sea snakes, but it was only her large black dreadlocks. Two elegant golden horns stood on her head, with a detailed crown perched on top. Around her thin neck was a necklace matching her crown. Her skin was as dark as chocolate with golden lines on her face, reminding me of marble. Those lines moved beneath her skin as if liquid gold flowed in her veins. On her right shoulder was a detailed tattoo I couldn't make out, but it looked like shells.

She had brown seaweed covering her breasts. Her tail glistened in various colors ranging from turquoise to blue to soft greens, depending on how the sea light caught it. Then, in her right hand, she held a golden staff with a snake wrapped around it. There was more detail at the top, ending with a sharp point. The tip part of the staff seemed empty, as if missing a part of it; there was fine golden detail that ended with the sharp spear.

And swimming around her was a gold and green moray eel with blue sparks shooting from it to the Queen. The blue sparks connecting it to its Queen reminded me of a leash on a dog.

"My Queen, wait—" Ossie started to say when she cut him off. Her eyes glowed golden, and she opened her mouth, spewing golden lava.

"No!" Ossie yelled, raising his hand. She closed her mouth, and her eyes bled back to its cool blue color. "Please," he said softer. "I'm not here to fight you, my Queen." Ossie moved away from the lava before it burned him. The lava sizzled, hardened, and sunk to the sea floor below our feet.

"What are you doing here?" The Queen demanded.

Her eel hissed as it swam around her, blue sparks continued flowing between them. "You threatened never to see me again."

I groaned inwardly. This was not the time for an ex-lover's tiff. I must've made a sound because one moment I was staring at the lava sinking, the next she's standing before me and about to open her mouth.

"Who are you?" she asked. Her dark eyes bleeding to golden.

"Don't hurt her," Ossie said. "She's important."

That caught the Queen's attention, and she decided against frying my skin with her potent golden lava spit. She neared and sniffed me. It was strange; her head moved out of the water protecting her and sniffed near my right ear. She moved back into the water as if pondering what I smelled like. Then, after a few seconds, her eyes widened and turned to Ossie.

"What is she doing here? She is never to be this far below the surface."

"Do you know where he is?"

"No."

"You're lying, Niriga. His dog sniffed him out, and he's here somewhere."

I flinched when I heard Ossie say her name, a name I'd never heard before but somehow knew how important it was. Niriga wasn't only the Queen of the Seven Seas but of all sea creatures. She ruled everything to do with water and knowing her true name was dangerous. I frowned at the thought; a thought that wasn't mine, yet I knew. I closed my eyes and sensed Vic; my father was here, and he was talking to me through the connection I didn't know we shared.

The Queen backed away as if Ossie had slapped her.

Ossie raised both hands in surrender, the scales shimmering metallic. "I mean no harm, my Queen, but Caesar picked up his scent. He is here—"

"He's ill," she said nervously, as if us knowing how gravely ill he was would be the end of her.

"We know," Ossie said, his shoulders sagging. "We need to speak with him." His tone was gentle.

"You can't." Her sea eel swam around her once more, pushing her farther away from us.

"We need to help him, Niriga," Ossie said her name again and the eel's blue sparks almost touched us. "We need him in order to find the Mask of Immortality."

Niriga neared and in a low voice, said, "I only meant for him to help but when I found him dying in his chambers, I had to take him and keep him safe. You see, he's the only one who knows where my pearl is," she raised her staff, confirming my suspicion that perhaps her pearl belonged in the empty spot, "and he won't divulge this information. Without this pearl, my power doesn't last."

"He was punishing you," Ossie said, standing taller. "You used your power to hurt others, and that's not what we do here. You used that pearl to fuel your own agenda."

Niriga averted her eyes in what I could only describe as shame. "I was young and stupid," she said, glancing up at Ossie with golden tears in her eyes. "I've learned my lesson."

"Are you up to speaking with him?" Ossie asked, staring at me. I nodded. "Good." Then he turned to Niriga. "Can she see him?"

She stared at me suspiciously. "Fine, but on one condition. I'll only set him free once I have my pearl back." She arched an eyebrow.

"We don't have time for this."

"There is no time here, Ossie. I want my pearl and in exchange, you can have him."

"You fight dirty."

"Don't we all?" she said.

"Fine," Ossie said. "We'll help get your pearl back and you'll free him."

"Deal," she said with satisfaction. "Now come with me so that you can ask him where my pearl is and retrieve it. But you," she pointed at Ossie, "stay here."

Ossie raised his hands in mock surrender. "No problem."

Chapter Twenty-Four

I followed Niriga down into the dark depths of the sea and my ears didn't block, nor did it feel like my head was about to explode from the pressure. When I no longer saw the others, I pulled my knife from behind my back and squeezed the hilt, making me feel better. I didn't know this Queen or what she was capable of, and I didn't want to find out—

"Here," she said, pulling me out of my thoughts. "Open the door and Victor, your father, should be on the bed." She stood on one side to let me through.

I narrowed my eyes at her. She said *'your father'* in such a way as if it were a warning or a threat. Either way, I was wary of her.

"It's safe, I promise you," she said. "I want your father alive. He is of no use to any of us dead. Besides, even if he's killed, his contracts remain. Nobody gets out of his contracts."

I didn't know that, and it was useful information.

"Thanks," I said, pushing the door open. Once through, the door slammed closed, making me flinch.

"Scout?" someone called from deep within the dimly lit room. "Is that you?" The figure stood up from the bed and approached.

"Father?" I closed the gap, almost slamming into him. I wrapped my arms around his waist and sighed. It was like coming home, but feeling his frail body against mine saddened me. "How are you feeling?" I asked, even though I could see how he battled.

"Strangely enough, I feel better down here," Victor said with a smile that didn't reach his eyes. His skin color was almost back but his hair remained white. "How did you get here?"

"Long story, but the short version is I landed in Os's arms in his room, and he took me to his brother, Ossie, in the Library."

Something flashed in Vic's eyes that I couldn't discern.

"Do you know them?"

"The demon brothers?" he said, glancing away. "I know them. They're good demons."

"I know. It's so strange. Anyway, they're helping me."

"Good… good… you're in excellent hands."

"Do you know where River and Zenon are?" I asked. "I thought they would be with you?"

"No, Niriga fetched me a while ago. I don't know where they are, but don't worry, they can't be far."

"Unfortunately," I glanced down, not wanting to look him in the eye when I said the next bit, "before we can help you, we need to free you from Niriga." I looked up at him when I asked him where the pearl was so she could free him.

"Of course. I should've known she'll never do anything

without wanting something in return." He exhaled deeply and his knees buckled, no longer able to hold his weight. I helped him back onto the bed so he could sit. Once he caught his breath, he turned his dark blue eyes on me. There was something he wanted to say, but he hesitated.

"What is it?" I asked, sitting beside him.

"It's…" he said, leaving his sentence hanging. He pulled me closer and kissed the top of my head. "Niriga's pearl is next door to your chambers. I know he scares you, but you're the only one who may enter. If anyone else goes inside, they'll never find their way back. Only you can retrieve it and leave unharmed."

"Are you referring to the door with the heavy lever?" I asked.

He nodded knowingly, as if sensing my fear. "I promise you, he won't harm you." He sat up, coughing.

I flinched as if he slapped me. I knew the room near mine very well; when I had first arrived at my father's place in the Underworld, I'd encountered the occupant by mistake. I'd stopped beside it to see if there was anyone inside, but let's just say the thing living in that room scared the bejesus out of me.

"Is this another one of your tests?" I asked, standing up and pacing. "I mean, you've done this before. Is it so that I can get my wings to grow?" My wings chose that moment to pop out through my clothing and flapped. I quickly hid them again, mildly embarrassed they were still so small.

"Scout," Vic said, patting the bed beside him, "it was only the one quest you had to go on. That was your initiation into the family, which you passed with flying colors. Whatever happens to you after that is just life. I no longer test you, but you pushing your own limits. And your wings will blossom when you stop thinking everything is a test."

I pursed my lips and fell onto the bed beside him. He winced in pain but said nothing. I thought about what he said, rounding my shoulders, and my wings popped out again.

"Yes, they are still small," he said, stroking them, "but when you change the way you think about them, they will grow, and you'll be able to use them." He coughed and wiped the blood off his lips with his hand.

The back of my throat hurt, watching him die in front of me. "Ossie says we need to get you out of here in order to retrieve the Mask of Immortality. Please don't die on me while I get the pearl."

"I'm not going anywhere," he smiled thinly. His eyes held unshed tears. I hugged my dad, hesitating to let go when he patted my shoulder. "It's time. Get the pearl so that we can find this mask." He held onto my ponytail for a moment before letting go.

I stood, but before I left, I turned to him. "So, all I have to do is enter the room, and that creature inside won't harm me?" He nodded. "And the pearl is there for me to see? It's not hidden anywhere?"

He grinned. "It's not hidden, but remember, nothing worthwhile is ever easy."

I grumbled to myself, but when I pecked his cheek, sadness and shame washed over me. I only had to do this one tiny thing to get the pearl back; it would ensure his release. He wasn't asking for much, and I knew I could do this. Once we had the pearl, Niriga would release Father, and Ossie could locate the Mask of Immortality. Easy.

When I headed for the exit, I glanced over my shoulder to see if he was still sitting, but he was already lying on his side, facing the other way, and barely breathing. It pained me to see him so fragile. When I closed the door gently behind me, I almost walked into Niriga.

"It didn't go well?" she asked, amused.

"No, it went swimmingly. It's what I have to do now that I don't like."

"Do you need help?" she asked, grinning. Her eel swam around her, and a blue spark slapped my shoulder, sending a bolt of pain through my body.

"Ow," I moaned, rubbing my arm, "that hurt."

The eel opened its mouth in such a manner it looked like it was smiling. If only I could poke a finger in its eye.

"Let's get you back. The sooner I get my pearl, the sooner we can help your father."

"How will you do that?" I asked as I levitated up with Niriga and she swam us to the others. I glanced down at my feet, and it looked like I was standing on glass, in the ocean, with the dark depths below me. It was surreal.

"I know where the magician's assistant is," Niriga said, smiling.

"What? Where? Why didn't you tell us sooner. We've been wasting time here when we could go after him."

"Shush, the less everybody else knows, the better for them. And besides, Ossie knows how to bring the mask to us. Once that happens, only then can we go after the assistant. Besides, he isn't a nice wizard, and we'll need your father strong to help defeat him."

The lines between my eyes deepened; I couldn't believe she just shushed me like I was her child. Feeling annoyed, I said, "I thought the assistant was human."

"That's what he wants you to believe, but everyone knows who the true showman is—"

"The assistant?"

"That's right. The magician is a brilliant performer, but

without his assistant, there is no magic. There is no magician and there is no show."

That would explain how the magician could do his tricks. It made sense. "But why is he doing this?"

"Someone commissioned him to do it. A higher supernatural is at play here, and everyone needs to be aware. If they destroy your father, there's no holding them back from coming after the rest of us."

"Do you know who it is?" I saw Caesar bounce up and down when he saw me, catching everybody's attention. The demon brothers turned to look at me as one while Julia smiled.

"No, but whoever it is, he... he isn't nice."

No shit, Sherlock, I thought as we approached everyone. Niriga was as helpful as she was unhelpful.

"See, everybody is still alive," Niriga said sarcastically. "Now let's get this over and done with so I can get on with my life." And with her parting words, she swam off into the distance with her eel swimming around and blue sparks shooting everywhere. When the eel swam around her and faced me, it smiled again. There was something wrong with that sea creature, but I would keep my thoughts to myself.

"Let's get out of here," Ossie said, heading for the exit. "Where do we have to go?"

"Dad's chambers." I sighed. I wasn't looking forward to going inside that room. Whatever was in there scared me.

Chapter Twenty-Five

"Are you sure you don't want my help?" Ossie asked with concern. He stood against the door, not allowing me to open it.

"Vic said only I could go in there," I said, pointing at the door near the bathroom and my room with the ancient metal and a slot that opened, and one could see only darkness inside. "If you enter, you'd never be able to find your way back again... only I can retrieve the pearl."

"Do you know who's inside?"

I shook my head. A wave of dread flooded my system. Going inside that room was like stepping on sinking stones in a crocodile river. One false move and I'd lose a limb.

"You can't go in there alone," he said. I appreciated Ossie's concern for my safety and was grateful that the other secret tomb pushed me in their direction. I didn't know what I'd do without either brother, but this was something only I could do.

"I'll be all right." I tried sounding convincing, but failed miserably.

"Just let her go," Os said behind me. He draped his arm over Julia's shoulders and kissed her temple. "If Victor says it's fine, then it's fine."

"Have you heard any stories about the occupant?" Ossie asked, sounding angry. I shook my head. "The stories going around the Underworld claim that once he starts hurting his victims, he doesn't know how to stop. He will find a way to hurt you."

I touched Ossie's chest and gently pushed him out of the way. He was huge and still in his scary demon form. I doubted my little nudge really made him move out of the way, but he did so willingly, anyway.

"I don't like this," Ossie grumbled.

"I know," I whispered. "Me either, but I must do this." I glanced up at him with pleading eyes; I had to do this alone.

I slid the slot open, and darkness greeted me. I waited a few seconds, but no demon with yellow eyes greeted me. No monster grunted beyond the door, nor did any creature slam up against the metal and scrape its nails down it.

I sucked in a deep breath of air and turned the handle; it squeaked beneath my touch but I didn't stop and turned it all the way until the lock clicked open. Moaning sounded on the other side of the door and Ossie's larger hand with black talons enveloped mine.

"I'll be okay," I said, patting his hand and smiling up at him. "I need to do this," I removed his hand from mine, "I have weapons and if all else fails, I'll push his soul out of his body."

"Shout if you need us." He nodded once. "I'll be right here."

"Thanks Ossie, you'll hear my screams," I said, trying for humor and once again I failed because nobody smiled—

I needed to work on my funny bones, or maybe the creature would suck on them in about ten minutes' time.

I opened the door, expecting a monster to jump onto me and rip out my throat. Instead, warm air greeted me and thick darkness.

"Hello," I said, my voice breaking. "I mean you no harm." I stepped inside the dark, cavernous room and gently closed the door.

Shuffling sounded behind me, and I pulled out a flash-light I had forgotten in my old room. When I left the Underworld last year, I didn't pack a bag; I just left, leaving items in my old room here. I was thankful for it, otherwise I wouldn't have a light to help me see inside this room.

I shone the light, turning around in a circle, but there was nothing much to see; everything was black and seemed to go on forever. The floor was dark, too, with a fine mist enveloping me.

I took another step forward. Victor had said the pearl would reveal itself when I entered, but there was nothing but darkness.

"Can you tell me where the pearl is?" I said, knowing someone or something was near, although I couldn't see them.

"Which one?" He whispered behind my right ear, sending a cascade of gooseflesh down the righthand side of my neck and back. It felt like a sharp blade cutting through my skin and I shuddered.

"Ah, uh, the one from the ocean... I mean, it's the one that belongs to the Queen of the Seven Seas."

A warm wind blew strands of my long hair, and I felt the weight of something going down my ponytail. "So pret-ty," he said, grabbing hold of my hair and yanking my head backward.

I winced, feeling the pain shoot down my neck. Praying silently to myself, I hoped he didn't like hair; I wanted it longer.

Another gentle wind blew against my naked neck, making all the hairs on my body stand at attention. The sensation was different here as I fought not to cringe and fighting the urge not to grab my knife and killing the monster behind me.

It would be easier for me to kill him, but I didn't know what the repercussions would be for Victor and thought it best not to do anything unless provoked—but if he continued pulling my hair I'd classify that as being provoked and would kill him.

"Let's make a deal," he said, now standing in front of me. His rancid breath assaulted my olfactory senses, and I covered my nose and mouth with one hand while raising the other hand holding the flashlight. The beam of light struck his dirty feet first and as I made my way up his soiled pants and shirt, I struggled to move farther up.

My hand shook, pointing the light at his chest; the torn shirt at the top, revealing his naked chest and tattoos of flames and naked women; they were in various stages of rape and torture. Tears welled in my eyes as bile rose up my throat. I didn't want to touch this man; I'd already seen a vision when I touched Os's hand and if the same thing happened now, touching this demon, I was sure my mind would crash in on itself.

"What's wrong?" he said, pulling me back to my strange reality. "Don't you like my tattoos?" He touched his chest with both dirty hands and started rubbing his pert nipples. He made a strange flicking sound with his tongue, and I dared not see his face.

The light shook in my hand and his breathing became

ragged until he finally grabbed his crotch and rubbed himself there. He panted as he rubbed and continued making sucking sounds.

I gagged when he blew out a breath; it smelled as if he'd eaten a rotten corpse. Then when the sounds of him rubbing himself and sucking on his lips, I wanted to run away and get Ossie's help, but I had to see this through. I gritted my teeth and waited patiently for him to finish.

When he finally finished, he wiped his soiled hands on his pant leg. His breathing quieted. "Thank you," he whispered sinisterly. "That was amazing. I haven't had company in so long I don't even know how long I've been here." He chuckled. "Oh yes, there's a reason you're here, isn't there. I guess... before I forget, you want the pearl. You can have it if you give me what I want."

I thought I had just given him what he wanted, but I wouldn't argue with him; he'd been alone for so long he was a little greedy. I squeezed my eyes tight, imagining what he wanted and closed my top tighter around my body.

He laughed loud and heartily. "No, not that, my dear. I've already sorted myself out with the essence of your perfume alone. What I want the most is something that will remain here with me. Something that will last for all eternity. I have had nothing pretty for so long, and since I can never have you... I think I'll have your hair instead."

No, no, no... not my hair. My shaky hand moved up toward his face, and I wished I hadn't. He smiled in the light, his teeth were sharp and pointy, his smile was broad and hungry. His skin was pale and scarred; like someone took a blade and scraped his skin over and over as it healed, and his bald head was dirty. But it was his eyes, or the lack thereof, that caught me off guard; the sockets were empty, and pus filled.

"I want your hair, and only then will I hand over the pearl," he said. His smile stretching from ear to ear. "If I can't wear it, I'll sleep with it." He leaned forward and breathed in, making my skin crawl. "You smell lovely, my dear. So delicious." His toothy grin left me on edge.

I grabbed my ponytail with my free hand and brought it over my shoulder. I loved my hair and had been growing it since I was a little girl, and enjoyed Mason brushing it for me before bedtime. He helped me with the knots and always bought the best shampoo to keep it soft. He said it was something that made me stand out from the other girls. My hair.

"Your hair will grow back," he said matter-of-factly. "Me, on the other hand, will never have hair." He rubbed his bald head, scratching at a scab, and pus oozed out, which he wiped away with the palm of his hand.

I exhaled a shaky breath, combing my fingers through my soft locks. It was only hair, and he was right, it would grow back. But... it was mine, and I had fond memories of Mason and me. Having long hair reminded me of him. If it was gone, I didn't know if those memories would remain.

I scowled as anger filled my veins at the thought of having to give up something that was mine. This was my hair, and it wasn't the only thing I was giving up. My life could be in danger, too. The moment I gave this demon my hair, he could easily kill me.

I quickly squashed the selfish thoughts; there were people counting on me, and there were demons outside who would help me the moment I screamed. I wasn't alone in this, and I'd always remember Mason. I would forever have him in my heart.

It was only hair...

Sticking the flashlight into my satchel with the beam of

light illuminating above me so that I could still see the scary demon, and reached for my weapon. I grabbed my ponytail by the elastic and raised my sharp knife.

"Yes, dear, that's it. Cut it… cut it off. Cut it and give it to me." His tone was sinister, almost animated.

I lowered my hand. "Show me the pearl or I'm not doing it. I need to know that you have it. I'm not giving you my hair for nothing."

He grunted his frustration. "Blasted girl. Must you ruin all my fun." He turned around and stomped into the thick darkness. Even with the light, I couldn't see where he went.

My shoulders sagged as the tension between my shoulder blades dissolved, but tensed again when I felt him behind me. I hated how he did that and silently cursed myself for not sensing his whereabouts.

I squeezed the hilt in my hand, ready to strike him in the gut, when his hand came in front of me holding a smooth, rounded object, lustrous and finely colored a gentle white. The large pearl glowed from within and silk moved beneath the surface. It sparkled in the dim light and continued moving. The pearl was alive, and I got the distinct impression it sensed me near it. The closer the man brought it to my face, the brighter it glowed.

"It likes you," he said behind me, his rancid breath blowing through my hair. I shuddered. "It never glows this brightly for anyone. Not even the Queen."

I opened my mouth to ask how he knew when he grabbed my ponytail.

"Now give me what's mine," he growled.

The next few seconds happened quickly and slowly and all at once; he dropped the pearl and grabbed my ponytail. I dropped the knife and reached for the pearl with both hands. The pearl landed in my hands safely, it was hard to the touch, and the sound of my hair being cut pierced my ears so loudly I felt it in my soul.

I fell forward but stepped just in time, avoiding a crash to the floor, and loose hair fell into my face. I swallowed my screams as tears filled my eyes as I cradled the pearl to my chest, feeling its heat beat against me. Spinning around, I pulled the flashlight out of my satchel and shined it on the demon.

He stood hunched over, holding my hair in his right hand, and a sharp talon extended in his left hand. His left hand morphed back into a hand, and I swallowed hard.

He brought the tuft of hair close to his nose and sniffed, the elastic keeping it together. Then he pressed it against his cheek. Purring sounded and his smile widened. "Beautiful, beautiful hair... thank you, my dear. Now leave!" He yelled the last two words and without taking a step, I picked up my knife, levitated toward the open door, and it slammed behind me.

Chapter Twenty-Six

"What did he do?" Ossie yelled, pulling me into a demon-bear-hug. "I'm so sorry, luv," he said into my short hair. "I'm sorry for what he's done to your beautiful hair."

I stood frozen against Ossie's chest, gripping the pearl in both hands. I was too afraid of letting the item go in case it disappeared and losing my hair would be for nothing.

"Scout? Talk to me," Ossie said. He leaned his chin on top of my head, still hugging me.

I opened my mouth but choked on my words. One tear slid down my cheek, and then another. My tears wet my cheeks and my unevenly cut hair stuck to my face. The tears could be of joy for surviving that monster, and for my hair. Whatever the reason, I allowed the emotions to take hold of me and then I would stop. My mom always said to get out whatever was bothering me. Rather out than in.

Hearing my cry made Ossie's embrace that much tighter, and I struggled to breathe. I double tapped him on his back. "Too tight."

Ossie let go of me and gently took the hair off my face. "Your hair, tiny human, it's gone," he said gently.

Then he said something to Os in demon language that made me glance up at him. His devil features frightened me; his eyes narrowed, his fists white-knuckled, and his jaw muscles ticked. The horns on his head turned red and steam came out of his fiery mouth. The veins in his neck and down his arms burst open with lava moving beneath the surface. Heat blasted me backward, and I almost smacked into the moving wall behind me, but Ossie caught me before I fell.

"Sorry," Os said, trying and failing to hide his anger. He rubbed his face, softening his sharp demonic features, but his ominous tone remained. "The boogeyman inside could've asked to be let go, yet he wanted your hair."

I exhaled a shaky breath, but no words came out. I felt like a scared sixteen-year-old instead of a young adult.

"It's ok," Julia said, coming to my side. "I can fix it." She lifted odd strands, then squeezed my neck. "Can I trim her hair somewhere?" she asked, looking at Os.

"We need to go," Os said, closing the gap.

"Give me five minutes, Os," Julia said, not backing down. If I wasn't mistaken, she actually grew an inch taller than Os.

Os raised his hands. "I'm not here to fight with you, my love, but we have to go. Victor is dying."

"Five minutes won't make a difference," Ossie said, coming to Julia's aid. "Besides, time is irrelevant anywhere in the Underworld."

"You too?" Os said, scowling at his brother.

"You know how beautiful her hair was, but now it's all choppy and untidy. The least we can do is help Scout feel good again," Ossie said nicely. "Now, instead of wasting time talking about it, give Julia a pair of scissors." His tone was harsher. "It will be quick, and then I'll get us back there in no time."

I smiled faintly when Os magically produced a pair of scissors and handed them to Julia. "Be quick," he grumbled and stormed down the hallway toward Father's living room area.

It amazed me that Os cared so much about Victor. I wondered whether Victor had tied them to his soul the way River was. If that were the case, then their lives were in grave danger, too. There were so many lives at stake and here I was fussing over hair that would grow back. Losing some hair was nothing compared to losing lives.

I watched Os keep himself busy in the living room and Ossie watching Julia and me while Caesar sat at my feet. I wondered where River was and hoped he too was okay, and I was sure Zenon was causing trouble wherever he was.

Julia smiled kindly and started fixing my hair. It took her only a few snips to get my bob straight at the back. With each cut, I watched my hair fall to the floor as the man from that room came into my mind's eye, holding my ponytail in his hand wearing that sinister smile. At least that's all he did. My hair would grow back. Although he frightened me, he didn't hurt me.

I shivered when a cool wind caressed my neck. I'd just stopped crying when a rogue tear escaped my left eye and rolled down my cheek.

"It's okay," Julia said, giving me a sideways hug. "Short hair suits you, too, and your hair will grow back."

"I know," I whispered, wiping the tear with the back of my hand. "It just happened so suddenly. He caught me off guard, and he," I glanced at the closed lever, remembering his awful breath on my skin, "was gross."

"It's over," Ossie said, reaching for my hand. "Let's go. We need Niriga to free Victor."

Chapter Twenty-Seven

Ossie got us back to the Ocean within seconds. My hand kept touching my naked neck and feeling the short hair. I was used to grabbing my ponytail, but now that there was nothing to hold, I kept feeling the bare skin of my neck, hoping my hair would magically reappear.

I couldn't remember the last time my hair was so short, but I knew it was something I could get used to; it was only hair. I sighed sadly as I followed Ossie through the door and into the ocean realm, then stopped dead.

An octopus ejected ink in thick spurts, and in the shape of its body, then it darted away. Another fish had its middle gutted with its insides spilling beside it, messing the water.

A shark approached, opening its mouth revealing no teeth; they had pulled its razor-sharp rows of teeth from its jaw, leaving nothing but blood and chunky raw meat. The shark stared at us knowingly; it wouldn't survive long.

The once blue ocean had lost its luster, and in its place a murky blackness had moved its way through the water like an oil spill, killing the coral reef, and leaving the sea anemones black. While maiming the fish, dolphins, and sharks to die and rot in the inkiness.

Even the smell of the salty water had evaporated and instead the smell of sulphur wafted around us.

"What is going on?" Ossie said, standing beside me with his enormous arms folded across his chest.

I glanced up at him; the demon was so big that his folded elbow came up to my eye level when he stood like that. My eyes flitted to his face and, for a moment, caught a familiarity I only noted now. Something flashed in my peripheral vision, and I glanced in that direction, searching for the light.

"Something is out there," Ossie said.

I squinted, assuming my mind was playing tricks on me when I saw it again. In the distance, among the blobs of blackness were dim blue sparks, followed by minimal movement. Niriga's moray eel closed the gap with something attached to it. As the eel got closer, I realized what it was. The Queen's golden staff was piercing its body like a fish kebab.

"Where is the Queen of the Seven Seas?" I asked nobody in particular. "Where's Victor…" I turned to Ossie and said, "We need to get down there and find Victor. Whoever did this had to be searching for him."

The moray eel sparked blue and swam down.

"I guess we follow the sea snake," Os said, standing on my other side.

"Moray eel." I corrected.

"Whatever," he said, grinning. "Ladies first."

We followed the dying eel to the same cave-like-room Niriga had taken me before. The door stood ajar, and someone had ransacked the room. The eel stopped near a pebble on the floor in the far corner and nudged the pebble with its nose. I crouched near the eel and picked up the pebble.

"Your father is over there." I flinched at the voice emitting from the pebble. I brought the stone closer to my face and inside swam Niriga; Queen of the Seven Seas. She was tiny and enclosed in a stony jail.

"How did you get inside there?"

"It was the magician's assistant," she grumbled, her face contorting into a scowl.

"Is he using the mask?"

"I don't know, but he's become more powerful than he was before, not only from the mask but he's also channeling his power from elsewhere." She thought for a moment, then added, "That type of power is familiar, yet I can't place it." She scrunched her face in disgust. "You must destroy him."

I wanted him gone, but first we needed the mask before we could think about destroying anyone. Once we had the mask, we could heal Victor, and then he could help destroy the assistant and anyone else involved. I turned toward the bed, but it was empty.

"Where's Victor?" I asked with alarm. My stomach dropped to my toes at the thought of his demise. I'd taken too long retrieving the pearl, and then Julia fixing my hair. We should've left my hair and hurried back here. We could've arrived on time to prevent all this. I sat on the bed with a heavy heart.

Ossie and Os stood nearby while Julia sat beside me.

"He's safe," Niriga said from her stone jail in my hands. "I locked him below to keep him safe," she said, pointing at the spot where I picked her up. "But hurry, he doesn't have much longer."

"Will this help you?" I asked, raising the pearl for her to see.

"No, but when Victor is well again, he'll free me from this place." She pressed her palms against the sides of her invisible pebble prison for effect.

Blue light caught my attention and the moray eel fell to the floor, dying.

"What can we do about him?" I asked, moving the pebble at such an angle she could see her fishy companion.

Niriga choked on her words, then after a moment she said, "Nothing. There's nothing anyone can do for him."

It saddened me to hear that. There were so many unnecessary deaths because of this stupid mask. There were some who put their egos and selfish needs above everyone else's, all in the name of power. In that moment, revenge consumed me, and I would do everything I could to destroy the assistant. But right now, I could only focus on one thing, and that was Victor. I had to get him out.

"How do I open the latch?"

Niriga didn't have time to respond. Ossie blew open the latch, sending sparks everywhere, water splashed and rippled in all directions.

"You could've killed him," I said, placing Niriga's pebble carefully on the bed beside Julia, got down onto my hands and knees, and crawled to the hole in the floor.

"Victor?" I called, placing my hands on either side of the hole and slowly bending inside, but darkness was all I saw. "Dad?" I called again, feeling my chest tighten and my throat ached when I swallowed. "Dad!" I yelled, leaning farther inside the dark hidey-hole. "Look what you've done." I gave Ossie the stink eye. "If you've killed my dad, I'll do everything in my power to hurt you."

The expression on Ossie's face made me feel bad for what I'd said. *Almost.*

Perhaps we were too late. That he was already gone long before Ossie blasted a hole in the floor. A loss I hadn't felt since Mason died crushed my lungs as I struggled to breathe. I choked on my next word, my voice soundless, and tears escaped as they brought feelings to the surface from a place I was avoiding. I sat back in defeat, wiping tears off my face, but new ones kept falling.

Someone coughed and a puff of dust emitted out of the hole; particles sparkled like diamonds near my face. I frowned, wondering whether they had reduced my father down to a husk filled with dust under the sea floor. I hated that blasted movie, yet I smiled at the fond memory of sitting with Mason, eating popcorn and enjoying *The Little Mermaid*. It would have been a better memory if I had spent that time with Victor, but I couldn't get everything I wanted.

There was another cough and another puff of dust. I fell onto my hands and knees once more, peering inside the deep, dark depths of the ocean floor.

Large red glowing eyes stared back at me, and they smiled. "You came back," Victor said, moving closer to the surface until I saw his face. He was still pale and gaunt, with a few additional bloody scratch marks on his face.

"It looks like you were in a war," I said, reaching for him.

"Your hair," he said sadly. "Your hair is short."

I reached for the short strands, staring at him with sadness.

"I didn't think he'd ask for your hair. I'm so sorry, Scout. Never would I have sent you to him knowing this."

"It's okay," I said, smiling, but it didn't reach my eyes.

"The important thing now is to get you out of here and find the assistant."

Before Victor could respond, Ossie and Os were by my side and grabbed Victor. They carefully pulled him out of the hole, then Ossie picked him up and carried him to the bed.

Julia held Niriga-the-Pebble, who was moaning about something, yet we couldn't hear her.

Victor's frail body seemed to shrink before my eyes.

"It's lovely to see you three working together and nobody is bleeding," Vic whispered. His smiling eyes flittered to Os, Ossie, and then me.

I didn't understand what he was getting at, but it wasn't important now. "We need to find the mask," I said, interrupting him. "Ossie found information in one tome in the Secret Tomb." I almost giggled at the way tome and tomb sounded, reminding me of how-now-brown-cow.

"Victor," Ossie spoke, pulling me out of my childish thought. "There's a way to bring the mask to us."

"How?" I asked, losing patience.

Ossie arched a dark demon eyebrow and continued speaking as if I never uttered a word. "You linked the mask to yourself when they used it against you. It will be difficult at first, but if you concentrate, you'll be able to call the mask to you."

Victor exhaled a relieved breath, and a thin smile played on his lips. "That's excellent, my boy. I knew you three could solve this. I knew it all along." He closed his eyes and began mumbling words I didn't recognize and surmised it was demon language. Sweat peppered his already damp forehead as he concentrated on his words. Him summoning the mask was such an obvious solution I didn't know why I didn't think of it sooner, but I didn't know enough about it to offer an opinion.

We stood around the bed watching Victor, and hope caressed my heart. This had to work. I never prayed, but I did then. While Father mumbled his words, I glanced at Ossie and Os with a questioning look. I didn't know what Victor meant by *'my boy'* and wanted answers, but before I uttered a word, lightning crashed, striking the bedside table, and the mask fell through a portal along with River.

Chapter Twenty-Eight

The mask fell in slow motion on the bed near Julia. She bolted up so quickly she disappeared, only to reappear behind Os. At least she still held Niriga-the-Pebble.

River bounced on the bed beside Victor, looking worse than he did before. His skin was paler than Vic's and he was incredibly thin; almost skeletal with a thin layer of translucent skin.

River's eyes flitted to mine; we stared at each other for what felt like minutes but it was only seconds. And during that glance, I felt so much. I felt the loss of our relationship, remorse that we didn't work harder to stay together, guilt that my father forced him to work under him, and all the love I still had for him yet couldn't express it. He was powerful yet withering away. In a blink of an eye, he could become dust himself.

I broke contact with River and stared at Victor, who didn't look great himself. The pain in my chest worsened, and I swallowed hard. I didn't like any of this. I didn't enjoy seeing the people I loved in pain and wilting. They were powerful supernaturals who were indispensable, yet this awful creation could do so much damage in such a short amount of time.

Slowly, I stood up and stared at the mask instead and the sadness eating away at me turned into anger and rage for an object I wanted desperately to destroy.

"Nobody touch it," Ossie said, staring at Victor. "Not even those who used it before. In the tome, I read that when you touch it, it takes power away making you mortal. If you touch it again, the new power becomes potent, making you crave more. If you keep touching it, it chips away at your humanity until there's nothing left of you but a mindless creature driven by greed and power. And then it will only kill you quicker—"

"No," Victor said, trying to shake his head, but winced instead. "That's wrong. If we use the mask again, it's meant to restore what it took."

"That's what they want you to think—"

"Then why call it back?" Victor asked.

"To restore power, you need to destroy it," Ossie said.

"Must only Victor destroy it, or can anyone?" I asked.

"It won't matter because it will restore everybody who is still alive back to their original form. It's like resetting a clock."

"Why didn't anyone do this before?" I asked with a grumble. "Idiots."

"Because they thought destroying it would be a bad idea. Not everyone has access to the information I have. But, luckily, once it's destroyed, it will reset. Unfortunately, the rumor started by someone spreading it and everyone thought the same thing. You know how those go," Ossie said, rolling his eyes.

"Here," Os said, handing Victor a baseball bat he'd conjured out of air.

I frowned. "Where did you just pull that from?"

Os grinned. "Luv, I'm a demon and can conjure anything I need. Even Julia can do it."

I looked at Julia and she wore a broad smile, snapped her fingers, and a milkshake appeared in her hands.

I licked dry lips. A milkshake would go nicely now. When all this was over, I'd be enjoying a lovely milkshake and waffle.

Victor groaned beside me, pulling my attention back to him. He held the baseball bat in both hands, raising his hands above his head and as he swung, the door blasted open with Myles filling the doorjamb.

Chapter Twenty-Nine

Well, I assumed it was Myles, the assistant, but he no longer resembled a human. He was a strange goblin-like-creature with dark green skin, long pointy ears on the sides of his head, a fat belly, hunching over himself and with the largest nose I'd ever seen. He also had tusks sticking out of the top and bottom lips.

I cocked my head to the side; he was an ogre, goblin and orc all rolled into one grotesque creature, still wearing Myles's coat. I shuddered at the thought and wondered whether his brain was still fully functioning or if the mask's power had taken over, leaving him nothing but an incoherent vessel for the parasite.

Myles grunted, sending plumes of smoke from his pierced nostrils. His teeth were sharp, thin, and pointy but extremely skew.

"Mine," he said, pointing at the mask on the bed and opened a case that was slung over his shoulders. I assumed he kept the mask there. "My mask." He pointed in the general direction of the mask and then at his case.

"You hurt people," I said. "I think it's only fair to take back what you stole."

"Must you aggravate the creature?" Ossie asked, pumping his arms as he readied to fight a monster almost as big as he was.

"Now isn't the time to moan at me, Ossie, now go get that green thing. I've had enough of him."

"Ask him who he's working for," Victor said, trying to stand.

"Did you hear?" Os said to Myles. "Who's your daddy?" he asked, chuckling.

Myles grumbled, then a piece of slimy snot dripped out of his left nostril.

"Ew, that's just gross," I said, glancing away. There was something about bodily fluids I didn't like, and that was one of them.

"What happened to you?" Ossie asked sincerely. "How many times did you touch the mask?" he said, closing the gap. "Didn't anyone tell you the more you play with your toys, the more deformed you'll become?"

I laughed at the comment, then quickly schooled my features when it turned its sights on me.

"Look at me, buddy," Ossie said, grabbing its attention again. His tone was deep and throaty, making all the hairs on my forearms pebble. "You're one ugly mother f—"

"Okay, that's enough swearing," I said, grabbing my knife. "Maybe sit down for a bit, Dad," I said, helping him sit again. "We first need to sort out this bozo." Once Victor sat, I stood beside Ossie.

"What do you think you're doing?" Ossie asked, pushing me backward. "This isn't a fight for little girls. Now stay over there where it's safer." He pointed in the far corner on the other side of the room.

"I can help," I groaned, pushing his muscular arm away from me.

"I'm sure you can, but I'd rather keep you safe for now. If he gets through me and Os, he's all yours."

"Ugh, thanks for nothing."

"We're f…" Ossie said, leaving his word empty.

"What?" I asked. "What do you mean? And don't tell me to wait, there is something you're keeping from me. Please, just tell me now." I glanced back at Victor, who wouldn't meet my eyes. "Dad? What does he mean?"

Victor sighed wearily. "They are your half-brothers, Scout."

I stared at him, trying to read his facial features while processing the information that I had demon half-brothers. I didn't know if that was a good or a bad thing, but it also didn't matter since I already had a vampire-were-leopard half-brother. Having demon half-brothers could be beneficial. I hoped.

Victor winced as he stood up slowly and cautiously approached. He wheezed as he breathed, each step taking more energy from him.

I groaned inwardly. "Why are you getting up again after I just got you seated? You're so stubborn." I shook my head in disappointment. "I can hear you just fine where you were."

Os flashed by his side to help him stay upright.

"These boys have suspected who their father and mother are," Victor said, glancing between us three. "When they found her diary in the library, they put the pieces together which confirmed their suspicions," he tapped Os's shoulder, then squeezed it, "then when most of the Under-world heard about you," he looked at me, "they realized they had a human sister."

Ossie and Myles growled at each other, oblivious to our conversation. Their behavior was very animalistic. Their growls became louder and louder as they readied to fight each other.

"Why didn't you tell me?" I asked with pleading eyes. "Why did I have to pry this out of you?" I surmised it was because he was on his deathbed and he'd rather I heard it from him than from the demon brothers.

"Nobody is supposed to know." He side eyed the demon brothers. "But there's always a time and place to share such important and personal information. And I didn't want you hearing it from someone else or getting hurt because of this information. I shouldn't even have children, but," he shrugged nonchalantly, "I guess I wanted them more than I thought." He smiled, and it reached his eyes, but then he collapsed. Luckily Os was there in time to lift him up.

I reached for him to help but Os waved me away yet giving me a look that said, *it's okay, I got this.*

Screaming behind me made me spin around, and I stood ready to defend myself. Myles charged Ossie, raising his makeshift axe. Ossie stepped backward, raising his arms and as Myles neared, his hands morphed into sledgehammers and slammed down as hard as he could, hitting him in the face and left shoulder, making his knees buckle.

Myles swung his axe down before hitting the ground, slicing Ossie's right inner thigh; liquid mercury blood oozed out of the wound. Ossie's black scales shimmered silver in the light. He hissed, then the wound stopped bleeding and closed.

Myles climbed to his feet, wiping the yellow blood from its bottom lip, and spat out a piece of its tusk. His eyes glowed yellow when he felt the wound on his shoulder but ignored it. He grunted, and more plumes of smoke emitted from his flaring nostrils.

I stood on one side so that I was out of the way and glanced between the fight and Father. The mask remained on the corner of the bed, with Julia still holding the pebble. While Os stood at Victor's side, keeping him up and protecting him.

Myles roared, spittle flying everywhere, and charged Ossie again. Ossie waited for the last second before getting out of the way and before he slammed into the wall, Ossie's hands morphed into miniature scythes.

My eyes widened and my jaw opened; Ossie was powerful, and I wondered what other weapons his hands could morph into.

Julia gasped at the sight as if this was the first time she'd seen Ossie's weapons, too.

Ossie moved his hand-scythes slowly and with purpose. He struck Myles in the chest and moved downward. The sharp blades sliced through the ogre-goblin-assistant easily; its thick hide splitting open, revealing yellow flesh beneath the dark green skin. He reminded me of a bright and juicy tropical fruit, except I wouldn't want to take a bite out of him.

Myles's ear-piercing screams shattered the mirror and cracks formed in the walls, followed by water dripping out of the largest crack. Yellow blood pooled at Myles's feet, and he slowly glanced up at Ossie with dark eyes that bled to black.

Ossie pumped arms, and the scythes disappeared. He stepped to the right and closed in on Myles.

"Stay back!" Myles screamed, raising his arm with palms facing Ossie. I doubted that would stop Ossie, but he didn't move. "Let me touch the mask. Give to me one more time."

If he touched that mask one more time, it might give him the power to smite Ossie out of the Underworld.

"I don't think so, abomination," Ossie said with a warning in his tone. "If you go near that mask, I'll destroy you before you can get there."

Myles touched the gaping wound that stretched from his chest down between his legs. I was sure if he had to open that wound with his hands, his insides would fall out. He took one step forward. Sweat peppered his forehead, and he wrinkled his nose. His face contorted, making him appear uglier than he was.

"Take one more step and I'll chop off your arms," Ossie said, raising his left arm for Myles to see the butcher's blade.

Myles glanced nervously at Ossie and just when I thought he would listen; he didn't, he lunged for the mask.

I watched how it all happened at once; the ogre-goblin-assistant jumped for the mask, Julia sat upright, and River dove. I screamed as Myles pushed Ossie away and was about to touch the mask.

Then my world stopped.

River got to the mask first and something happened; he disappeared inside the mask when Myles touched it with his crooked finger. But before he could use the mask's power, Victor smashed the mask with the baseball bat.

Then my world went black.

Chapter Thirty

My world winked into nothing. The darkness was so thick I could feel it between my fingers and brush against my face. The feeling was intense yet light, as if I walked through sticky clouds. When I opened my eyes and focused on the living room in Victor's home in the Underworld, Victor stood beside me in his former, powerful, glory with my demon half-brothers on my other side, and Julia holding Os's hand and the pebble still in her other hand.

We stood in a circle as if in prayer, and in the middle of our circle bubbled the leftover chunks of the assistant with bits of broken wood mixed in.

"That's disgusting," Julia said, stepping away from the circle and sitting down, pulling Os beside her.

"Oh, my gods," Victor said, stretching his body. "That's the worst thing that's ever happened to me." He arched backward, stretching his spine. Then he rolled his shoulders and clicked his neck. He seemed to be fine, and his hair was once again as dark as night.

I squinted at the chunky assistant bubbling on the floor,

at something sticking out from inside of his coat. Leaning forward, I carefully removed a card; it was a ticket to see the magician in 1988.

"What's that?" Victor asked.

"Just a small memento," I said, pocketing the ticket.

Footsteps echoed down the corridor and Zenon appeared, looking like he just stepped out of a GQ Magazine.

"Where have you been?" I asked.

"Stuck down here while you play with the demons," he quipped and stopped beside Victor. "What in gods name is that? Ugh, it's bubbling." He kicked the slime, and it messed his boot, forcing him to bend down and wipe it with a hand-kerchief.

My nose wrinkled. Zenon never used a handkerchief, and I wondered whether Léon's habits had rubbed off on him.

"What?" Zenon asked, staring at me.

"Nothing, it's just I've never seen you use a man-cloth before."

"Not always," he said, looking for a trashcan to throw the slimed item away. "But they do come in handy." He dusted his hands.

I shook my head in shame. River had disappeared inside the mask that Victor destroyed, and here I was chatting about my brother's handkerchief.

"Victor—"

"I know," Victor said, pulling me in for an embrace. I flinched. He rarely hugged, but I wrapped my arms around his waist and pressed my ear against his chest and allowed the rhythm of his heartbeat to soothe my aching heart.

"Where did River go?" I mumbled into his chest. "Why didn't it heal him like you?"

Victor sighed. "I don't know, but I won't rest until I find out who's behind this and where he is."

I raised my head off his chest and stared into his dark blue eyes. "Find him," I said as a rogue tear escaped, and I left it to fall down my cheek. I wanted my father to see the hurt I was going through. I loved River. Yes, we had broken up, but I still cared for him; I still loved him.

"I'll do everything I can," he said lovingly, brushing another tear off my cheek.

"Don't wait, please. Find out where he went now."

He nodded. "I will."

"What happened?" Zenon asked.

"The assistant is mush," Ossie said, "and River disappeared inside the mask the moment Victor destroyed it."

"Shit, talk about bad timing."

"Zenon!" I yelled. "Don't be so insensitive." I mumbled into Victor's chest.

"Sorry," he said, holding his hands up in surrender. "Sorry, sister." He stroked my back.

Victor moved slightly, as if uncomfortable, and I took it as a sign to let him go. I stood beside him and wiped my eyes dry.

"And these two are my half-brothers too," I said, pointing at the demons.

Zenon gawked at them, then quickly schooled his features. "Right," he said, his eyes flitting to Victor and back to the brothers. "Your father has been quite the busy one." He grinned.

Julia raised her hand, pinching the pebble between her thumb and index finger. "Um, Victor, Niriga is asking for help," she said, waving the pebble.

"Oh yes, give her here," Victor said, taking the pebble from Julia. He held the pebble in his hands and blew on it.

Freezing cold air whipped past my face, and the air buzzed and sparked. The pebble in his hands vibrated until it got so large, forcing Victor to drop it to the floor. The moment it struck the carpet, Niriga popped out with water drenching her clothing and splashing across the floor.

"That took you long enough," Niriga mumbled, unappreciatively. "Now my pearl, please," she said, holding out her hand.

Victor nodded, and I handed it to her. She carefully took it out of my hands and cradled it against her chest. The pearl shining brightly, but not as bright as when I held it.

"I'll need to make a new staff to put this in," she said sadly. Then glanced up at us one by one with a weak smile. "I hope the ocean hasn't been completely destroyed by that idiot assistant." She shook her head. "I'll try to salvage what's left." Hope filled her words as she pushed her shoulders back and raised her chin. "Thank you," she said to Victor, bowing low, then disappeared.

"Do you think she'll be able to restore order to the ocean?" I asked.

"Definitely, otherwise I wouldn't have put her in charge," Victor said. "Now, go home to your mother while I tend to business here."

Chapter Thirty-One

Three Weeks Later

I stirred my porridge with a spoon until the cinnamon was mixed, then I added swirls of honey, enough to make the three bears jealous.

"Are you coming with us?" Mom asked, sitting across the table. She finished her coffee and placed the mug in front of her. Her eyes boring holes into my soul.

I dropped the spoon and it clanked against the glass bowl. I sat back, folding my arms across my chest.

Mom mimicked me.

I scowled. She did too.

"What are you two doing?" Ralph asked, plonking his big bum beside me, but I didn't greet him.

"She's still grumpy—"

"Mourning Mom, I'm in mourning. There's a difference."

"No, Scout, you're wallowing in misery." Blaire usually called me cute names like pumpkin or sweetie-pie. When she used my real name, it meant I'd pissed her off. "And it's time you got back on your feet."

"Dad hasn't found River—"

"He's looking, Scout," she interrupted. Her frown remained on her face as she continued staring hard at me. The lines between her eyes deepening. When I glanced away, she continued talking. "And you know he will do whatever he can to find River." Her words were gentler, softer. "At least he is well enough to look. Imagine if he too had disappeared. Then what?"

I hadn't thought of that. My father was alive and well, and I was grateful, but sadness kept taking over. I glanced at her when tears welled in my eyes, and I vowed not to cry today, yet I couldn't help it and wiped my face and sniffed.

"My darling," Mom said, her tone softer, gentler, reminding me of days when I was ill and had to stay in bed. "I know you're hurting, but there are monsters out there that need destroying. And we need you. We're a team; you, me, and Ralph." She pointed at me, then Ralph, and then herself.

The silence stretched between us and Ralph shifted uncomfortably in his seat beside me.

"It's a doozy," Ralph said, pulling out a rolled up yellow folder from the large fanny pack he now wore around his waist and read the assignment. "It's another police request," he leafed through the pages, "and it's a boogeyman-type-creature praying on the homeless."

Mom groaned. "Where?" She stood up and poured herself another cup of coffee.

"Near one of Léon's nightclubs." Ralph read the top of a page and grimaced. "It's quite gory. It poisons them before half eating them."

"Humans or supernaturals?" Mom asked, standing against the counter sipping her coffee.

"Both," he said, paging through the folder.

"Is it just the one nightclub?" I asked, hoping by interacting with the case I could get my mind off losing River. He was out there. I could feel him. I just didn't know where to look. My throat ached when I swallowed the lump of emotions that had been building up.

Regret was an awful emotion that, if one didn't let go, it could manifest itself into something dark, heavy, and may lead to a life of despair. At that moment, I decided that when I saw River again, I would tell him how I felt. That I missed him and wanted to be with him. That I wanted us to try again. We loved each other, and we deserved a second chance. We had to try.

"Yes, the murders seem to happen at only one place by the river and forest," Ralph said, bringing me out of my thoughts once more. "And it's near the warehouse where Kai and Lee live."

"We should pay them a visit," Mom said, placing her mug on the counter. "They might have heard something. But before we go, what are we allowed to do with the monster when we catch it?"

"Destroy," Ralph said gravely. "I doubt any jail could hold it anyway if what it does to the bodies is to go by. Quite vile," he raised the photos for us to see and I had to glance away. I hated it when Ralph showed us the gruesome crime photos. It was our job to understand what had happened, but sometimes he didn't bother warning us, he just shoved it under our faces to shock us.

He placed the latest crime scene photos on the table near my bowl and I lost my appetite; the bowl of oats and the mushed brains on the sidewalk were enough to make

179

anyone think twice about eating. In another photo, the victim's chest cavity had melted away, as if the predator's spit was acid.

I sighed. At least my mind was not on River for the last three minutes. I stood up from the table and Mom wrapped her arm around my shoulders, pressing her head gently against mine.

"Help us catch this one," she said. "You'll see. The busier you are, the quicker time flies, and by the time Victor finds River, you'll be ready."

I patted her arm. "Let me get changed and I'll see you outside." I left the two to talk behind my back and closed my bedroom door behind me.

I lived with Mom and Léon in his Labyrinth of a home. Before Zenon was born, Léon extended his home to accommodate us. Zenon's bedroom was across the hallway from mine, but he wasn't home; he was gallivanting across the globe in search of an artifact thought to reverse the effects of aging. We're still waiting to hear where he was.

Undressing, I grabbed the body armor suit Victor had given me and pulled it on. My black wings had grown a little more since I helped Father. The wingspan was now at least a meter each. They weren't big enough for me to fly high and far, but it encouraged me they would grow.

I rounded my shoulders, and the wings disappeared into my shoulder blades. I pulled the armor over my arms, and it melded with my body like a second skin.

Mom called from downstairs.

I yelled I was almost done. Once dressed, I opened my bedroom door to rush down, but I smacked into a wall of muscle. Léon stood like the dangerous vampire he was with a knowing smile. I glanced up into his deep blue colored eyes and smiled. It was the first time these three weeks I'd seen Léon. He'd been busy with vampire problems with Sebastian.

"How are you?" he asked, his tone still had that velvety touch but because I was kind of his daughter, his words didn't make me want to wet my panties. Thank goodness he wasn't a pervert.

"I'm fine and you?" I grinned.

"Good," he said, that knowing smile still tugging at his lips.

"Do you want to talk about that day?" I was referencing Zenon and my back to the past moment, trying to find the Mask of Immortality.

"No, only to thank you."

"Oh, why is that?"

"I guess," he started, glancing up as he thought. "That it's made me appreciate Blaire, you and Zenon a little more now."

I smiled. "Thank you, Léon. That's very nice of you to say."

"Come, Scout!" Mom yelled from the bottom of the stairs.

"Anyway, go before your mom yells at me too," he said, chuckling.

"See you later," I said, waving as I descended the stairs.

"Au revoir, ma chérie," he said, turning on his heel and heading in the opposite direction with his arms behind his back and his head raised. Forever the Prince of Darkness, even when nobody else was around to see him.

Ralph knocked on the warehouse door that was owned by

Léon and guarded by four shifters; Kai, Lee, Flynn and Jude.

Lee opened the door wearing a smile and the tiniest shorts I'd ever seen him wear. His tanned muscular body was magnificent to look at; especially for a young lady such as myself; I was twenty-three and allowed to look. I didn't always touch.

"Hey, what's up?" he asked, glancing left and right as if we had an army with us. "Should I be worried you three are here?"

"No, but we have a few questions," Mom said.

"For you, Blaire, anything." Lee grinned, showing off his boyish good looks in a rugged way with his unkempt hair and chin stubble.

"Have you heard about the murders taking place at *Fangs & Friends*?"

Lee's smile dropped. "Yeah," he said solemnly. "Gruesome really. Jude and I found one of the victims three nights ago." He stared off into the distance, deep in thought. "Is that why you're here?" He glanced at Mom and Ralph.

"Yes, we're here to destroy the monster."

"Good, we haven't been able to go anywhere near that part of the forest since this started happening."

"Is it only near the river?" I asked, thinking of something.

"Could be," Lee said, thinking. "I know others have been deeper into the forest that side, but it was on the other side of the river. So yeah, could be near the river that feeds into the small lagoon or the lagoon itself."

Mom glanced at me and shrugged. "Why do you ask that?"

"It's just a hunch," I said, pointing. "Let's go. If it's the monster I'm thinking of, we'll find it by the lagoon."

We walked the three blocks, passed *Fangs & Friends*, and headed for the path leading toward the lagoon. I'd only been at this club once and knew that most patrons frequented the lagoon for midnight skinny dipping.

"How do you know to come here?" Mom asked. Her tone was accusatory.

I continued walking ahead, pushing low branches out of my way. "I've only been here once before, but everyone knows where to go when looking for an extra good time."

Mom made a strange noise, but I didn't want to turn around to see her facial expression. I knew she wasn't happy; which I didn't understand. I was in my twenties. I'd already had one boyfriend, and already killed more monsters before my twenty-third birthday than she ever did. Yet knowing where the lagoon was had upset her.

I ignored her and continued on. I traversed down two wooden steps, rounded a thorny corner and walked between two bushes and the sparkling blue lagoon came into view. The late morning sunlight struck the rippling water at such an angle, making it shine like diamonds.

"Not too close," Ralph warned. "Something is swimming beneath the surface." He pointed at a dark spot in the far corner, then it moved closer and stopped in the middle of the lagoon.

I stood on the edge of the water, ensuring it didn't wet my shoes, and watched the ripples slap against the sand, reminding me of the ocean. The sun was warm against my face and a light breeze blew through my short hair.

I glanced up, and the darkness remained in the middle of the lagoon. Ralph and Mom stood behind me. I focused on the water creeping closer to my shoes, one small wave after the next. Something glistened beneath the surface. It was round and possibly a silver coin. I bent down to pick it up when someone grabbed me from behind, yanking me to the left.

The creature screamed as it swiped at my face, but instead of scratching my eye out, it only struck air. Like a bad horror movie, the foul smelling, two-armed man with two legs had six heads where there should only be one and each identical face turned on me.

I was expecting a creature that had a body of a dragon with snakeheads. Instead, he was human-like, with six necks and heads competing with each other to take control of the arms and legs. He struggled out of the water and walking on the soft sand made it worse for him. His knees buckled, but he managed to stay upright. He walked a few steps then knocked his shoulder on a low branch, which only pissed him off and the hydra-heads each exhaled and a smelly green gas escaped each open mouth.

"What the hell is this thing?" Ralph asked, pulling me to my feet.

"It's a Hydra," I said, out of breath, "or more specifically, the Lernaean Hydra."

"Why all the heads?" Mom asked, aiming both guns at the creature.

"Each time someone cuts off a head, two grow in its place."

"Shit."

"Swear word." I moaned as I pulled my knife from its sheath.

"How do we stop it?" Ralph asked, holding a knife and a gun.

At least we were armed, but now we needed a flame thrower. I glanced around, looking for something.

The Hydra snapped its toothy jaws and approached

Mom. She backtracked slowly, keeping it in her sights while Ralph followed closely.

"We need to cut off its heads and cauterize the wound before more heads grow back," I whispered to Ralph. "I don't suppose you have a flame thrower in your fanny pack?"

"I wish, but I have a lighter," Ralph said, moving closely with the creature.

"Hand it here and when I tell you, start chopping off heads."

Ralph dug in his fanny pack for the lighter and threw it at me without glancing away from the Hydra.

"Any time now," Mom said nervously. She moved through the dense bushes and trees.

The creature had set its sights on Mom and no matter how many times I threw broken tree branches at it to get its attention, it still wouldn't look at me.

I flicked the lighter, and it just sparked. It took three tries before the flame caught. I held my sharp blade over the flame, heating it.

Mom and Ralph moved deeper into the forest with the creature and its foul breath closing the gap. I wasn't sure if trying to push its soul out of its body would help, but with six heads, I was sure it would try to eat me before I could do anything. And I wasn't sure how its breath would affect me once I got close to it.

As I heated the knife, I stared at its heads and necks for an easy way Ralph could cut them while I tried to cauterize the wounds to stop two more heads from growing.

"Ralph," I yelled. "Will your knife be sharp enough to cut through everything at once?"

"Of course," he yelled, still concentrating on the creature, "I sharpened it this morning." He waved his blade in the air for me to see.

"Just in case you meet something you need to chop up?" I yelled, feeling the hot blade with my finger and burning my skin. "Crap," I cursed when a blister formed.

"Hurry, you two, I can't do this forever." Mom was squeezing her body between two thick trees.

The Hydra leaped in the air for Mom. I screamed for Ralph to get to him before he could hurt her. Mom fell backward and scrambled on her bum to get away from it. The creature slammed its shoulders into the two trees and its six heads pushed through the gap, each trying to take control of the body.

Ralph cut through the first two necks, severing the heads before I could get to him. As I neared, four heads popped in place.

"You need to be faster, Scout," Ralph said, wiping sweat off his forehead with his forearm. "And stand closer."

"Quickly," I yelled, "before it turns around and attacks us." The moment the words left my mouth, I cringed. The creature stopped struggling through the two trees and turned around. Half of the heads stared at Ralph, the rest at me.

I swallowed hard. I didn't know what to do first. Cut it with my knife and try to push its soul out of its body or wait for Ralph to slice and dice while I heated the knife again.

We didn't get the chance to do any of that. The Hydra lunged for Ralph. I stepped backward, dropped the lighter, and waited to see what it was going to do.

Ralph swung the blade down, slicing through its shoulder and severing its right arm. Mom came around the other side and started shooting at its heads.

I joined the party by gripping its left arm and pushing my right hand into its chest. Cringing at the sensation of its body against my palm, I pushed harder. Its soul edged out of its back only an inch, then it bounced back. I was about to push harder when its soul pushed through the front and all heads snapped their toothy jaws at me.

"We need to find another way," I said, pushing its body away from me and pushing its soul back in, but it wasn't working. Whatever this thing was could control its soul; that thought alone made my skin crawl with goosebumps.

Ralph picked up his lighter, held it in his left hand while slicing through some necks with the blade. Once the heads were off, he pressed the flames against the wounds, but it wasn't hot enough to stop more heads from sprouting.

"Shit!" Ralph yelled when eight more heads popped out. The creature was a bouquet of heads now and each of them was angry or hungry or both; *hangry*.

"We need help," Mom said, fending off the Hydra who was now trying to stomp on her with its enormous feet. He was like an elephant with those thick ankles and broad, flat feet.

Mom fell to the floor. The Hydra lunged for her.

"Blaire!" Ralph yelled, leaping onto the creature's back.

My voice got stuck in my throat watching this thing attack my mother. I only had one mother, and nobody could ever replace her. As if I didn't have enough drama in my life. First, it was Victor who had almost died, River who was missing, and now this creature was hurting my mother.

Anger flooded my veins. No creature should hurt my mom. She was my mom. There were many things we needed to do together still and now that I was working with her, our relationship was great. I loved working with her.

Using my fiery anger, I channeled my father's powers; it was something I hadn't done before for fear of what it would do to me. He was dangerously powerful, and I was afraid that if I used it, it would consume me. But seeing this thing reaching for my mother with all those hungry heads, I had to do something.

His powers washed over me like a bucket of hot water, and it felt as if I grew taller. I opened my eyes and glanced down at my hands and long, black talons grew. I rounded my shoulders and my large black wings flapped behind me; they were at least six meters each.

I smiled.

The heads turned in my direction; their expressions changing from hunger to fear.

Ralph stopped stabbing the creatures back to look at me while Mom gasped.

"Scout?" Mom said, pushing the Hydra's foot off her thigh. The creature almost toppled over but corrected itself with its only arm.

I didn't want to wait for the creature to take in a breath and decide what it's going to do to us, so I lunged for it with my mouth wide open. My tongue was hot as I screamed and grabbed the Hydra by its shoulders; and with one talon, I sliced through the necks as if I were a laser, and before two heads could grow back; I breathed over each wound.

I flinched when I realized I was the one breathing flames and cauterizing the wounds, but then a wide smile stretched my face in two.

"No," Mom said, shaking her head, "that's too much scary happiness. Stop smiling and finish this thing."

I nodded, and slowly moved my sharp talon through its soft flesh, watching its last head scream in agony and that it was the last head. Once the head popped off, I breathed fire over its wound and pushed its body away from me.

We watched the Hydra tumble down the hill and get knocked around by each tree trunk or fallen log in its way until it eventually rolled onto the sandy part near the lagoon.

Then, as if today wasn't freaky enough, a beautiful sea creature crawling on its forearms, glancing up at us and winked, then quickly dragged the corpse into the water.

"I wonder if the Hydra was bothering the mermaids?" Ralph asked, picking up his fallen weapons.

"Probably," I said, sighing. "But where the hell did that thing come from and why now?"

"Maybe the Underworld left a gate open," Mom said, dusting herself off and combing her fingers through her dirty hair.

I glanced at her with my mouth wide open. She may be right. It reminded me of the demon-goat that wanted us to open the door at the time-loop secret tomb.

"Your wings, my darling," Mom said, closing the gap. "You've got your wings." She danced around me, fluffing my feathers.

My smile reached my eyes as I glanced over my shoulders at the large black wings and exhaled with relief. "Finally," I said. "I've been waiting so long—"

"Good job, kiddo," Ralph said, pulling me in for a sideways hug, careful not to bump my wings. "I'm so proud of you." He beamed like a father would to his child.

It warmed my heart to feel the love and appreciation from my mother and the people in our lives; they were our family. We didn't always get along and we fought, but at the end of the day, we loved each other.

"This calls for a celebration," Mom said, slapping my back. "What do you feel like doing?"

"I still haven't—"

Lightning struck a tree nearby, and I froze, along with my words. Angry wind whipped our hair and our clothing billowed. The air snapped and popped.

"Victor," Mom whispered beside me.

As she said his name, he appeared like the dark, scary devil he was. He stood in his black, shimmering armor, red horns, and sinister face; his eyes on me. He was probably angry that I channeled his powers, and now he wanted to punish me.

A nervousness I hadn't felt since that first time I met him made my hands cold and damp. My heart raced in my ribs, and I hid my wings. I lowered my head and averted my eyes. I mouthed the words, *'I'm sorry'* and hoped he heard.

"There's nothing to be sorry about, Scout," Victor said, touching my chin with his thumb and index finger, raising my head. "I'm very proud of what you did, and I've said before, my power is your power. I'm glad you did it, otherwise one or all of you would be dead."

He brought me in for an embrace, his large black wings closing around us, and in that moment, I felt loved and cherished. That the Lord of the Underworld loved me enough to keep me as his daughter, and that he felt pride.

I exhaled against his body and he chuckled; the low rumbling of his chest against my cheek. "I'm glad you're content, little one. But don't rest for too long. We need to go."

That caught my attention, and I glanced up at him, stepping out of his embrace. "What do you mean?"

"I know where River is—"

I screamed with joy. "Where?" I asked, wiping tears off my face.

"A place where only you can go."

I didn't like the sound of it, but if there was a chance I could help River, then I'd do it. "Okay, where?"

"Antarctica."

Next in the Scout Thorne Series

vinci-books.com/murdercrows

In a battle against time, some truths are better left undiscovered.

After River disappears, Scout's life spirals. But when her father uncovers his whereabouts in a remote Antarctic town, Scout must confront deadly creatures and a River who no longer remembers her. To save him, they must seek out Mother Nature herself—and unlock a world of secrets.

Turn the page for a free preview…

Murder of Crows: Chapter One

"What do you mean Antarctica?" I said, not understanding how River arrived there or who had left him there. He had disappeared while we were in the Underworld. Him being in Antarctica made little sense.

"The same reason, Scout," Dad said with a hint of sarcasm. "The person responsible for wanting me dead wanted River out of the way."

"But why?"

"Because together, he and I are stronger."

I pursed my lips. Someone wanted my father dead, and it wasn't just the assistant. Someone had hired the assistant to do his dirty work for him. I shook my head in shame. I'd been so focused on River and his disappearance that I didn't ask Victor if he ever found out who had started it all.

"Do you know who tried to destroy you?"

Mom stood closer, folding her arms across her chest. She stopped near my left-hand side and slightly in front of me in a protective stance. I didn't think she wanted me to leave with Victor again, and suspected every time he visited a trigger reaction occurred and she became a fussy-mother-hen over me. I didn't blame her, each time he took me away from her, it was for long periods of time.

"I thought you said you shared your power with River and now with me. Do we take power away from you, or does it just double?" I needed to understand what Vic meant and the only way was to ask like a five-year-old.

Victor rounded his shoulders, and his eyes flitted from Ralph to Mom, and then to me. He exhaled a breath, and I suspected he'd filled that sigh with annoyance.

"I've never shared this with anyone," he said gravely, staring down at me with intense eyes. "And if either of you," he pointed at Mom and Ralph, "say a word to anyone, I will destroy you."

"Stop threatening my family," I said, grabbing his index finger and lowering his hand. "Nobody will say anything. Now tell us." I was about to roll my eyes when Dad's features turned sinisterly and then returned to his devilish human demeanor.

"Whomever I share my power with doubles my power, and when we use it together, it's that much more powerful. My brothers and sisters hate that I can do this because none of them can."

"You mean they can't share their powers with anyone?" I asked, intrigued.

"No," Vic said, his shoulders dropping slightly. "And because of this, I always have a target on my back."

"Would your family hurt you?" Mom asked.

"Definitely. Seth tried to kill me when I was an infant. Our sister almost drowned me. But the point is, it could be either of them or something else entirely who used the Mask of Immortality against me. And now they have River..." he fell silent for a moment. His metallic armor twinkled as the shadows from the branches and leaves moved across his chest like ghostly fingers trying to touch him.

The waterfall in the distance slapped harder against the water's surface, pulling my attention away from Victor. I leaned on my left leg and peered around Father's broad shoulders and black wings and flinched.

A mermaid sat beneath the spray of the waterfall and washed his body. He had long, knotted hair and large, dark eyes. When he glanced up, he smiled; his enormous mouth had sharp teeth, and he blew a kiss before diving into the water.

"Scout?" Victor said, pulling me back into the present.

"Yeah?" I glanced up and smiled.

Victor glanced over his shoulder. "What are you looking at?"

"Just the mermaid who was there." I pointed at the spot where he was.

"Don't antagonize the water creatures, they don't play fair." He warned. "Anyway, you need to go to Antarctica—"

"No," Mom said, with anger in her voice. "I forbid it."

"Mom," I said, crossing the distance between us and wrapping my arms around her shoulders. "I'll be fine. You know I'll be fine, and you know I must do this."

"Why can't you go?" she asked Victor, ignoring me, but she still put her arms around me and squeezed me tightly against her body.

"You know I don't do well with humans or other supernaturals."

Mom snorted. "Yeah, true, especially with your temper tantrums."

I glanced up to see Dad's features morph into his more evil look, and then he calmed down.

"See, you can't even handle me teasing you."

"Exactly, Blaire, I have demons who do the dirty work for me."

"Does that include your own daughter—"

"Mom!"

She patted my shoulder. "It's okay, honey. The adults are having a conversation."

I pushed away from her and stood beside Dad.

"You know she wants to find River, so I'm giving her the opportunity. If I send my demons to find him, they always cause chaos. The last thing we need is another war between us or worse, they kill River. This way, if Scout goes by herself, she'll do so quietly."

"I'll be okay, Mom, I promise." I smiled, but she wasn't looking at me. She was glaring daggers at Dad.

"I hate this, Scout. You aren't ready to do all this by yourself."

"I know you want to keep me safe, but you know I can handle anything that comes my way."

She glanced at me, cocking her head to the side, and raised an eyebrow.

"If you aren't back by the end of the week, we'll join you and phone me every single day, or I'm flying out there to bring you home."

"Fine," I said. But what I didn't say was I'd do anything not to have her in my face while trying to do something on my own. My mom meant well, but sometimes her love smothered me.

She gave me a long hug and kissed my cheek. Ralph hugged me too and patted the top of my head; I swiped his hand away before he could do that a second time.

"Ready?" Dad asked, holding out his elbow for me to take.

"Sure," I took his arm, and we walked together toward the lagoon. We approached the lapping crystal-blue water when three heads popped up, each mermaid smiling. But instead of entering the water, we stepped out onto the freezing snow.

Grab your copy…
vinci-books.com/murdercrows

About the Author

A Multi-genre author writing twisted endings...

N Gray is a USA Today Bestselling Author who lives in Cape Town, South Africa, with her daughter and adopted cat named Miss Beans.

During the day, she's an analyst and provider profiler for a medical insurance company. At night, she types on her curved keyboard, creating fictional characters some may love and others you want to kill yourself.

She writes in four genres: urban fantasy, thriller, horror, and paranormal romance.

She now writes under Natalie Michaels for her new thrillers and SD Syns for her new horrors.

Acknowledgments

Thank you to my readers, old and new, for taking a chance on my books.

You are the reason I write the stories I do. As long as you keep reading, I'll keep writing.

I'm truly humbled by your support and encouragement.

I write in as many genres as I love reading in. There are so many stories swarming inside my head that I could never just choose one.

Horror is my guilty pleasure. I love writing short stories filled with dark humour and the occult with a twist ending.

Urban fantasy and paranormal romance are where I love to spend my time, and I have so many books planned that I don't have enough time (*but I'll get there*).

And lastly, my thrillers. Who doesn't love sitting on the edge of their seat while reading about what goes on inside the antagonist's mind? Well, I love writing about them.